Don't miss these other spellbinding novels by
DONNA GRANT

ROGUES OF SCOTLAND SERIES

The Craving
The Hunger
The Tempted
The Seduced

CHIASSON SERIES

Wild Fever
Wild Dream
Wild Need

DARK KING SERIES

Dark Heat
Darkest Flame
Fire Rising
Burning Desire
Hot Blooded

DARK WARRIOR SERIES

Midnight's Master
Midnight's Lover
Midnight's Seduction
Midnight's Warrior
Midnight's Kiss
Midnight's Captive
Midnight's Temptation
Midnight's Promise
Midnight's Surrender

DARK SWORD SERIES

Dangerous Highlander
Forbidden Highlander
Wicked Highlander
Untamed Highlander
Shadow Highlander
Darkest Highlander

SHIELD SERIES

A Dark Guardian
A Kind of Magic
A Dark Seduction
A Forbidden Temptation
A Warrior's Heart

DRUIDS GLEN SERIES

Highland Mist
Highland Nights
Highland Dawn
Highland Fires
Highland Magic
Dragonfyre

SISTERS OF MAGIC TRILOGY

Shadow Magic
Echoes of Magic
Dangerous Magic

Stand Alone Stories

Savage Moon (ebook novella)
Forever Mine (ebook novella)
Mutual Desire

And look for more anticipated novels from Donna Grant

Night's Blaze (Dark Kings)
Moon Thrall (LaRue)
Wild Flame (Chiasson)

coming soon!

THE SEDUCED

ROGUES OF SCOTLAND

DONNA GRANT

THE SEDUCED

© 2015 by DL Grant, LLC
Excerpt from *Moon Thrall* copyright © 2015 by Donna Grant

Cover design © 2014 by Leah Suttle

ISBN 10: 1942017162
ISBN 13: 978-1942017165

Available in ebook and print editions

www.DonnaGrant.com

ACKNOWLEDGEMENTS

A special thanks goes out to my wonderful team that helps me get these books out. Hats off to my editor, Chelle Olsen, and cover design extraordinaire, Leah Suttle. Thank you both for helping me to keep my crazy schedule and keeping me sane!

There's no way I could do any of this without my amazing family – Steve, Gillian, and Connor – thanks for putting up with my hectic schedule and for knowing when it was time that I got out of the house. And special nod to the Grant pets – all five – who have no problem laying on the keyboard to let me know it's time for a break.

Last but not least, my readers. You have my eternal gratitude for the amazing support you show me and my books. Y'all rock my world. Stay tuned at the end of this story for a sneak peek of *Moon Thrall*, LaRue book 2 out April 13, 2015. Enjoy!

xoxo
Donna

PROLOGUE

Highlands of Scotland
Summer, 1427

Daman Thacker sat atop his mount as silent as the rugged mountains around him. He looked over at the men he considered brothers – Morcant and Stefan.

As usual, the three waited on the fourth man of their group, Ronan. Ronan was the carefree one of them, the one who did what he wanted, dismissing the consequences. It was a hell of a way to live.

Oh, how Daman wished he could follow in Ronan's footsteps.

Stefan's horse snorted, shaking his great head, which caused Stefan to pat the steed's neck. The valley between the two mountains was wide. The summer sun was warm, with a breeze gently rushing past.

Above them, the shrill cry of a golden eagle broke the silence. Stefan glanced up, but Daman was scanning the ridge of the mountains. He smiled as he caught sight of Ronan.

Ronan's horse whinnied loudly, causing Stefan and Morcant to look toward the top of the mountain. Daman shared a smile with Morcant before Stefan glanced his way.

Ronan's horse pawed the ground, and a moment later, Ronan leaned forward. His horse raced down the mountain. Daman laughed along with Morcant. Ronan's wildness was just one of many reasons they had become friends, brothers.

It had begun a decade earlier when they happened to meet during a Highland Games. Their bond of friendship formed quickly and tightly during those few days, and not even the fact that they belonged to different clans kept them from meeting regularly.

As the years went by, their bond solidified into a brotherhood that nothing - and no one - could break.

Daman's mount danced sideways, eager to run, as Morcant finally got control of his horse and Ronan arrived.

"About time," Stefan grumbled.

Ronan raised his brow. "You might want to rein in that temper, my friend. We're going to be around beautiful women this night. Women require smiles and sweet words. No' furrowed brows."

Daman and Morcant's laughter didn't bother

Stefan since he was used to such words from them. Still, Stefan shot Ronan a humorless look.

"Aye, we've heard enough about this Ana," Daman said as he turned his mount alongside Ronan's. "Take me to this gypsy beauty so I can see her for myself."

Ronan's lips compressed. "You think to take her from me?"

Daman and Ronan had played this game before. It wasn't in any of them to even think about trying to take away one of their women. But it was always a fun jest.

Daman's confident smile grew as his eyes twinkled in merriment. "Is she that beautiful?"

"Just you try," Ronan dared, only half jesting.

"Be cautious, Ronan. You wrong a gypsy and they'll curse you. No' sure we should be meddling with such people," Morcant said as he shoved his hair out of his eyes.

Morcant wasn't usually the voice of reason of the four, but his comment had Daman's smile fading. The gypsies weren't allowed to remain in one place for long. Many clans would prevent them from crossing onto their lands if they knew they were coming.

The gypsies might be beautiful, but they were dangerous, as well.

Ronan laughed at Morcant and reined in his mount. "Ah, but with such a willing body, how am I to refuse Ana? Come, my friends, and let us enjoy the bounty that awaits." He gave a short whistle and his horse surged forward in a run again.

Daman's steed blew out a breath, anxious to run, as well. The three remained behind for a moment while Ronan took the lead as he always did. Each had found their place within their small group that had formed so long ago during the Highland Games.

"I'm no' missing this," Morcant said and gave his stallion his head. The horse immediately took off.

Daman and Stefan shared a look, and as one, they nudged their mounts into a run. It wasn't long before they caught up with Morcant.

Ronan looked over his shoulder, a wide smile on his face. He spurred his mount faster. Morcant then leaned low over his stallion's neck until he pulled up alongside Ronan.

Daman watched as Stefan's horse closed the last bit of distance and came even with Ronan. Daman gave his mount his head and rode up beside Morcant.

A few moments later, Ronan sat up and gave a gentle tug on the reins, easing his stallion into a canter. Daman and the others followed suit as they rode their horses four abreast.

Daman loved being with his friends, riding across their untamed homeland. Why then did he have a bad feeling about going to the gypsies?

There would be no stopping Ronan. Daman learned long ago that once Ronan had the bit in his mouth, he was going for what he wanted.

Then again, they all had their issues. Morcant's was women. He loved women — all women. That had gotten him into trouble more times than Daman could remember.

For Stefan, it was his anger. He oft times called it a monster, and when it took him, Stefan became someone else.

Daman had his own hindrance. It was his inability to ask for help – from anyone, even the men he thought of as brothers. It began when he was three and stealing food just to survive. He wanted more of a life for himself, and he wanted to do it all on his own.

It took years, but Daman was no longer homeless or starving. He was prized for his sword arm and often requested by his laird in times of need.

The four rode from one glen to another until Ronan finally slowed his horse further to a walk. They stopped atop the next hill and looked down at a circle of gypsy wagons hidden in the wooded vale below.

Daman looked at the caravan and the gypsies walking around. There was a large fire in the middle of the camp. Daman searched but saw no other Highlanders with the gypsies. His ominous feeling continued to grow, and he couldn't hold off letting the others know.

He shifted atop his mouth. "I've a bad feeling. We shouldna be here."

Morcant's horse flung up his head, and he brought his mount under control with soft words. "I've a need to sink my rod betwixt willing thighs. If you doona wish to partake, Daman, then doona, but you willna be stopping me."

"Nor me," Ronan said.

Daman waited for several moments as Stefan sat silently. Then, he gave Ronan a nod of agreement.

Daman wasn't surprised, but at least he'd told the others what he was feeling. Ronan was the first to ride down the hill to the camp, with Morcant right on his heels. Stefan galloped his horse down the hill as a young beauty with long, black hair came running out to greet Ronan in her brightly colored skirts.

Ronan pulled his horse to a halt and jumped off with a smile as Ana launched herself into his arms. Ronan caught her and brought his lips down to hers.

Stefan halted on Morcant's left side, and Daman rode up on Morcant's right. Daman glanced around, noting how the gypsies watched Ana with Ronan.

Ronan and Ana spoke quietly before Ronan turned her toward them. "Ana, these are my friends, Daman, Morcant, and Stefan," he said, pointing to each of them in turn.

Her smile was wide as she held her arm out to the circle of wagons. "Welcome to our camp."

Morcant quickly dismounted and dropped the reins to allow his horse to graze freely. He then walked between two wagons and into the center of the camp.

Stefan dismounted and patted his horse. "I'll be back," he mumbled and followed Morcant.

Indecision warred within Daman. The four of them were always fully invested in whatever they did, but for some reason, he couldn't walk into the camp. His gut churned with apprehension.

That's when he saw Morcant and Stefan exchange a look before they both glanced back at him. Daman slid from his horse and gathered the reins of all four mounts to tether them together.

"I'll keep watch," Daman said. He walked to an oak outside of the camp and sat.

Ronan wrapped an arm around Ana and walked away with her, saying, "Your loss."

Morcant gave a nod and continued to a woman sitting on the steps to her wagon, her bright turquoise and yellow skirts dipping between her legs while she braided a leather halter for a horse.

It was long moments before Stefan walked to the fire in the middle of camp and nodded to the three men sitting there.

Daman let out a sigh. Trouble was coming on swift wings. He knew it as certainly as he knew he would die in battle.

~ ~ ~

Daman scratched his jaw and ignored the thunder and lightning that had been on display over the mountains for the past half hour. The knot in his gut about the gypsy camp only intensified the longer he was there.

Something bad was going to happen. He knew it just as surely as he knew the storm coming in would last for an entire day. The sooner Ronan, Stefan, and Morcant were finished, the better.

Daman wouldn't make the mistake of returning with his friends again. And he would do his best to prevent them from coming back, as well. Perhaps a talk with the gypsies was in order. They were on his clan's land.

Three hours had already passed. It was time for him and his friends to leave. Daman rose and walked between the wagons to get their attention. Then he paused.

In the middle of the camp was a large fire, and many of the gypsies were sitting around it. Two were playing the violin, a hauntingly eerie song that somehow kept time with the thunder. Among the gypsies was Stefan, who stared into the fire as if searching for something. An old woman sat off by herself, her gaze on the wagon Ronan had entered hours ago.

Unease prickled Daman's skin.

He wanted to leave, but he wasn't going to go without his friends. Some unknown, unnamable emotion was coursing through him. Every instinct told him they needed to leave. Immediately.

Daman rose and walked to the edge of the camp. He looked at the ground, then up at the wagon where Ronan and Ana were. He could shout out Ronan's name, but his friend wouldn't answer even if he heard him.

Daman's gaze slid to Stefan. With Morcant busy, he could get Stefan's attention, but Stefan was talking to three gypsy males. Besides, Daman didn't need help. All he had to do was cross the boundary and get his friends.

He looked up at the sky and stared at the thousands of stars. The moon was only a sliver in the night, leaving the land cloaked in darkness. Daman ran a hand through his hair and returned to the tree where he'd been sitting. He'd wait for his friends as long as it took. Then he'd get them away.

No sooner had the thought crossed his mind, when the night was shattered by an anguished scream. It was filled with despair and fury dragged from the depths of Hell itself.

Daman's blood ran cold because he knew his apprehensions were becoming fact. He looked from Stefan at the fire to Ana's wagon where Ronan was exiting. Hand on the hilt of his sword, Ronan stood shirtless and looked at an old woman who stared at something in the grass.

Daman reached the edge of the camp when Morcant exited a wagon still fastening his kilt. Something bad was coming for them.

Daman searched the ground where Ronan and the old woman were looking. The bright pink and blue skirts of Ana, Ronan's lover, were visible from the dim light of the fire. As was the dagger sticking out of Ana's stomach.

The odds of any of them getting out of the gypsy camp without a fight weren't in their favor. By the looks exchanged amongst the gypsies, they were prepared to die to avenge Ana – despite the fact Ronan hadn't killed her.

Daman looked to Morcant and Stefan and saw

a slight nod of Stefan's head. Morcant slowly began to pull his sword from his scabbard as Ronan shook his head in denial.

"Ronan," Stefan said urgently as he palmed the hilt of his sword and waited.

There was a moment of silence, as if the world held its breath.

Then the old woman let loose a shriek and pointed her gnarled finger at Ronan. Ronan's eyes widened in confusion and anger.

Daman heard a gypsy near him whisper a name – Ilinca – as he stared at the old woman. Ilinca's face was contorted with grief and rage.

Words, hurried and unfamiliar, fell from Ilinca's lips. The language was Romany, and by the way Ilinca's dark eyes narrowed with contempt, it was a curse she was putting on Ronan.

Daman waited for Ronan to grab his sword and the battle to begin. When nothing happened, Daman looked harder and realized that Ronan was being held against his will. His pale green eyes were wide with confusion.

Daman opened his mouth to shout to the others, but Stefan drew his sword the same time Morcant rushed Ilinca. The old gypsy shifted her gaze to Morcant, and he halted awkwardly, her words seemingly freezing him in place.

Once it appeared Morcant was taken care of, her gaze returned to Ronan and she continued speaking in the strange language.

"Stefan!" Daman shouted.

But it was too late. Stefan's fury had been let

loose, the monster was free. Stefan released a battle cry and leapt over the fire toward Ilinca. He hadn't gotten two steps before the old gypsy pinned him with a look that jerked him to a halt instantly.

Then the old woman's gaze turned to Daman. He sighed and thought of his friends. There was one rule between the four of them – they lived or died together. Daman stepped over the boundary and a cold tremor rushed down his spine at Ilinca's triumphant smile.

He was immediately surrounded by men. Undeterred, Daman left his sword in the scabbard and used his dirk and his hands to slice, stab, punch, and kick anyone stupid enough to get close.

Five men fell – two dead. He put another three on the ground before he found his limbs immobilized. No matter how hard he tried to move his body, he couldn't.

The men parted, and Ilinca walked to him. Daman looked around, but Ronan, Morcant, and Stefan were gone – vanished as if they were never there.

He glared down at the old woman. He desperately wanted to tell her how he was going to kill every last gypsy he came across as punishment for what she had done to his friends, but the words wouldn't come. Ilinca controlled every bit of him.

"Why didn't you enter the camp with your friends?" Ilinca asked him.

His eyes narrowed as he realized she had allowed him the ability to speak. She wanted answers, but he wasn't going to give them to her.

His lip curved in a sneer.

"I shouldn't expect you would answer. Even if I would help you, you wouldn't ask for it, would you? Too proud, like so many others. Your friends have been cursed, but you probably already knew that." Ilinca drew in a breath and looked him over closely. "Why did you have to come into camp? You were wise enough to keep out earlier."

Daman saw her hands shaking. Her eyes were bright with unshed tears. She was upset by Ana's death, but he was desperate to find his friends. Even if it meant talking to her. "Where are the others?"

"Someplace they can't hurt anyone or themselves."

"Ronan didna kill Ana."

Ilinca lifted her chin. "He may not have stuck the blade in her, but he's still responsible. Just as Morcant is responsible for bedding an innocent and ruining the chance to align our people."

Daman tried to move his arms, but she still held him in place. "And Stefan?"

"You know the answer to that better than anyone else here. That one's rage is what got him cursed."

"What are you going to do with me?"

The old woman stepped closer and the gypsies closed in around her. "I had a vision a week ago of this very night, though I didn't see my granddaughter's death. I knew the four of you would have something important to do."

"Do? I'm no' important."

"I can only repeat what I know. What I saw." Her shoulders drooped. "My magic will ensure each of you reach your destination. What you do there is up to you. You can be freed. Or you can spend eternity in your prison. The choice is yours, and your actions will determine the outcome."

"I'm going to find my friends," he stated.

Illinca's lips pressed together briefly. She held up an amulet. "The next time you see this, your destiny will be before you. The path you choose will seal your fate."

Daman got that bad feeling again as Ilinca placed her hand on his forehead. He wanted to jerk away, but she still held him frozen. His eyes grew heavy, and the more he fought to keep them open, the more tired he became.

"Don't fight it," Ilinca's voice whispered in his head.

It was in his nature to fight. He fought as hard as he could against whatever she was doing to him, but it was too much. The world went black in an instant, like the snap of someone's fingers.

Ilinca sighed as she dropped her hands and took a step back from Daman. Then she nodded, and the men carried him to her wagon and brought him inside. Grief rose up in her like a tidal wave. She would tend to Daman later. Right now, she needed to bury her granddaughter.

Once that was done, she had a destination to reach.

"Grandmother?"

Ilinca held out her arms for Ana's younger

sister. When Amalia wrapped her arms around her, Ilinca held her tight. "It's almost over, my sweet."

"You didn't say Ana would die."

"I didn't know." Ilinca didn't stop the tears from falling. "Ana was impetuous and kind, but she wasn't as strong as you are."

Amalia looked up at her. "Where did you send those men?"

"Far away."

"And the fourth? Why didn't you send him, too?"

Ilinca glanced at her wagon. "Because he's the key to all of it."

CHAPTER ONE

MacKay Clan
1609

Innes stood in the great hall of the castle staring at their dwindling clan. Every day more and more people left. Not that she blamed them. People were starving, and with most of the warriors dead, their clan was weak.

She fingered the amulet hidden beneath her gown. It had been placed around her neck when she was just seven summers. Her mother had told her to never take it off. It had been passed down through their family for over two hundred years.

"You may need it one day, Innes," her mother said.

"Need it how? It's just a pendant."

"It's not just any piece of jewelry, sweetling. It possesses magic. There is a warrior hidden on this land. He's sleeping,

waiting for the time when we need him most."

Innes had thought her mother was making it all up until she was shown the sleeping warrior the next day. From that moment on, rarely a week passed when she didn't go see him.

Her brother's voice boomed through the hall as he tried to quiet everyone. Innes knew they were in trouble. There had been an attack in their forest by a lone man who had killed several of their men, as well as the defection of another clan member to their enemy, the Sinclairs.

"Enough!" Alistair shouted. He ran a hand through his dark hair, his nostrils flaring. "We will survive. We were a great clan once, and we will be again."

"What of Donald?" someone shouted.

Innes watched her brother's hands fist at his sides. It infuriated him that Donald was making more trouble for the clan instead of helping. Then again, their brother wanted to lead. Donald's pride was hurt from not winning the clan's support to become laird.

Alistair met her gaze, and she gave him a nod. She normally didn't take sides with her brothers, but in this, she wholeheartedly agreed with Alistair.

"My brother will be brought to heel," Alistair said, his words ringing clear and loud through the great hall. "Family or not, he is destroying this clan. I vowed to rebuild us, and I'll no' stop until I do."

The talk then turned to the stores of food for winter. Innes turned and walked from the castle. She made her way down the castle steps to the bailey, which was so quiet it was eerie.

It used to be one of her favorite places. All the noise, all the people. It was a central place for the clan. Now, it was a reminder of all they had lost.

Innes walked through a hidden postern door and out of the safety of the castle. They had only one man standing watch at the gatehouse, but she didn't want anyone to know where she was going.

A cool wind whipped around her as she walked across the land, reminding her in not so subtle a fashion that winter would soon be upon them. Their food stores were alarmingly low. The men who would be out hunting were now dead thanks to her youngest brother.

Donald had always been impetuous. He'd always been jealous of Alistair as well, but he seemed to realize that Alistair would be the one to lead. Over the past few months, however, Donald had become increasingly argumentative. He questioned Alistair's every decision and command.

Then, to her horror, he began to sway some of the remaining younger men to his side, claiming he would set things right one way or another. Donald's idea of *setting things right* was to attack the Sinclairs. Unfortunately, that idea turned into action.

It was a stupid, thoughtless move. The Sinclair clan wasn't only large, they were powerful. Their laird had several castles on his land being held by commanding, formidable men.

Donald thought he could attack Ravensclyde to see how strong their new lord – Ronan Galt – was, but he and his men had been put in their place quick enough.

How she wished that had been the end of it. Donald and his remaining men returned to the castle to heal and lick their wounds, and her brother swore to both her and Alistair that he would never attempt to oust Alistair again.

Yet, three days ago, he'd done just that.

Innes continued over the rocky landscape and up a steep hill. She had to lift her heavy skirts on the way up. Thunder rumbled as dark clouds rolled in. The air was heavy with the scent of rain.

She hurried down the opposite side of the slope hoping to beat the rain. Half way down, the sky opened up and drenched her. Innes didn't slow as she reached the valley and took a quick left into a grove of trees where the cave was hidden.

Once inside the cave, she stopped to catch her breath. Innes wiped away the wet strands of dark hair sticking to her face.

Just yesterday, she had been to see the warrior as she had every day since Donald had begun to push against Alistair's rule. But last night, she found no rest as her thoughts jumbled into what was happening and the possible outcomes.

She didn't need a torch to see the way. She knew where every stone was, where every hole lay. Her heart began to pound and her stomach twisted into knots when she walked down the narrow, twisting tunnel that eventually opened up to a small cavern.

A slab of stone sat in the middle of the cavern,

and upon that slab slept the warrior. Magic had kept him ageless and sleeping for two hundred years, just as magic kept the torches spaced evenly along the walls lit.

She didn't know what had happened to put him in such a situation. Her mother hadn't known either. The truth of that part of the story was forgotten long ago– or never stated.

Innes walked around the man. He looked so peaceful, so content. Through the years, she had come to him often and spoke of her worries and her dreams. Without realizing it, he had helped her get through some of the worst times in her life.

She had always thought him handsome with his long, wavy mane of golden hair and his rippling muscles. But a few years ago, she began to...long to touch him.

The first time, she barely laid a finger on him before she snatched her hand back. Eventually, she came to need to feel his skin beneath hers, no matter how innocent the touch.

Innes walked to him and rested her hands upon his upper arm, feeling the strength, the hard muscle beneath her palms. Feeling his warmth.

She took a deep breath and slowly released it as she let her gaze wander over his face. Unable to stop herself, Innes caressed her finger over his wide forehead and down the slope of his nose. She brushed across his square chin and along the hard angles of his jaw up to his sharp cheekbones. She traced the blond brows that slashed over his eyes.

Her gaze lowered to his mouth. She leaned

closer, rested her hand on the side of his face and outlined the shape of his wide lips with the pad of her thumb.

"I think I've come to need you," she said into the quiet. "That's not good. If everything goes according to Alistair's plans, I'll be married after the first of the year. I'm sure my new husband won't approve of the time I spend with you, talking and...touching."

She glanced down at his chest. His saffron shirt used to be closed, but she had parted it the year before to see more of his impressive chest.

"I'm your guardian," she continued. "And yet, I feel as if you're the one who has been watching over me." She dropped her forehead onto his chest and squeezed her eyes closed. "Donald did it again. He took some of his men out into the woods to attack the people of Ravensclyde, but he stumbled across a man that nearly wiped them out. Donald has gone out for a second attack, and I fear if Alistair doesn't do something soon, Donald will be the ruin of us."

She paused and raised her head to look at him again. Innes straightened and took his large hand in hers. "My mother says you're a great warrior. That one day you'll be the answer to our prayers."

Her heart knocked against her ribs at what she was contemplating doing. With her chest heaving and her blood running cold through her veins, Innes squeezed his hand between hers.

"I was told that I should only think of waking you under the direst of circumstances. Our clan is starving, and our numbers are rapidly shrinking. Other clans are eyeing our lands because we don't have enough warriors to fight. I think that's pretty dire."

She wiped at her eyes with the back of her hand. Once she revived him, there was no sending him back to sleep. He would be awake, his will once more his own. His life had been paused while he slept, and when he woke, he would once again begin to age like everyone else.

"I pray this is the right thing to do. Alistair is doing everything he can, so now it's my turn." She pulled the amulet from beneath her gown and then over her head. Innes looked at the silver piece, the markings faded from being held so many times. "Alistair is a good man, but he needs help. Please be that help for us."

Innes held the amulet for a few moments longer, debating on whether to leave without waking him, but the fate of her clan was at stake.

"Please be the answer we need," she whispered and gently placed her lips over his.

Innes set the amulet in his palm and closed his fingers over it just as her mother had instructed. She leaned back and waited, hoping he would wake immediately, but as the minutes passed without movement, she began to doubt.

She removed the amulet and put it in his other hand. Still nothing happened.

"Of course," she said and shook her head ruefully. "It would've been too easy to be able to wake you and have you save the day. Keep the amulet. I don't know why my family was bade to watch over you, or why you're in this cave, but I hope someday you get to wake."

Innes jumped when thunder boomed so close that the ground shook. Pebbles and dirt rained down from the ceiling of the cave. She glanced at the man to see him still asleep. Utterly defeated, she turned and ran out of the cave and back to the castle.

~ ~ ~

The sweet voice was back. Daman drifted upon nothingness, but every once in awhile he heard a woman's voice. He hadn't been able to hear the words at first. It was just sound, a calming, reassuring sound that he sought. Then the words became clear, as if she were right next to him.

It felt like an eternity in-between the times he heard her. Immeasurable time stretched endlessly before him. He didn't know her name, didn't know her face or why she was with him, but he felt...comforted whenever she was near.

It wasn't just her voice that affected him. It was her touch, as well. How he longed for more, craved more of her soft caresses.

She only ever touched his arms, face, and chest. Yet he yearned for her to go lower, to take his cock in hand. But she never did.

The sadness in her voice this time gave him pause. As did the part where she'd said he was supposed to help her. Help her how? He didn't even know who he was or why he couldn't seem to wake from the endless sleep.

He suddenly needed to know why her family kept watch over him, and why she thought putting something in his hand would wake him.

She'd mentioned marriage. He didn't want her to marry and never touch him again. He needed to see her face, to know her name.

To run his hands over her skin as she had done to his countless times.

He wanted to know the color of her hair and eyes, to see her smile. Most importantly, he wanted to be the one who saved her clan.

For the first time, he really fought against the strain of sleep. The warm metal in his hand heated, and his fingers gripped it tighter.

It felt as if he were swimming in a sea of tar. Every time he tried to surface, it yanked him back. But he kept swimming, kept struggling.

He kept her voice running through his head. His skin tingled from the memory of her touch.

Then, he saw the faintest pinprick of light. He fought even harder against the tide pulling him under, keeping him asleep. The more he struggled, the more the light grew.

Suddenly, his eyes snapped open and he sucked in a mouthful of air. He sat up, looking around for the woman. But his eyes only found an empty cavern, dimly lit from torches along the walls.

He looked down at his hand and opened his fingers. The moment his gaze locked on the amulet, he recognized it.

"The next time you see this, your destiny will be before you. The path you choose will seal your fate."

The old woman's voice was loud in his mind as her words replayed. What path did she mean? To him he had but one – to help the woman who came to him.

The question was: who was the woman, and where did he find her?

CHAPTER TWO

Innes had changed her gown and was drying her hair with a cloth when there was a knock at her chamber door followed by Alistair's voice saying her name.

"Come in," she bade and turned to face the door.

He took in her appearance and raised a brow. "You disappeared again."

"You had things under control."

Alistair looked at her with the dark eyes of their ancestry and sank into the chair next to the hearth. "I already have one sibling against me. It looks good to have you there. Shows your support."

"I was there," she argued. "Everyone saw me."

"Where did you go?"

He had asked so many times, and despite the fact she had never told him, he kept asking. "I needed to collect my thoughts," she answered.

"And what if Donald was out there?"

Innes spread the cloth next to the fire so it would dry and gave her eldest brother a droll look. "Donald wouldn't hurt me."

"Just as I thought he'd never go against me." Alistair propped his elbow on the arm of the chair and leaned his face against his fist. "He's no' returned, Innes."

She sat at his feet, tucking her legs beneath her. "And you're afraid if you send a party out looking for him that they'll either end up dead by Donald's hand or the men from Ravensclyde."

"Aye." He sighed heavily, his shoulders drooping. "Why did Da try to steal the sheep back with just a handful of men? Why didna he take me or Donald with him? Maybe then he wouldna be dead."

"You can't think that way. Da went without you because he knew it would be dangerous. He was trying to protect you. And he knew you would lead the clan if anything were to happen to him."

Alistair spread his arms around him. "Clan? Have you seen the people? More leave each day. I'm surprised another clan hasna come to take our lands by now. The only thing keeping them away is the threat of Ravensclyde descending upon us."

"So what do we do? Do we hand over our lands?"

Alistair cut her a look. "Of course no'."

"Then quit complaining and start figuring out a way out of this."

"I have."

The way he said those two words, with determination and regret, brought chills of foreboding to Innes. She knew exactly what Alistair was referring to. Marriage.

Everyone in their family sacrificed for the clan. She was just one of many, so there was no need to rant or cry about it. Especially if it saved the clan.

"Who will I marry?"

Alistair moved to sit beside her on the floor. He took her hand in his, while his dark eyes searched hers. "I doona want to do this."

"I know. You must do what you can for our people."

"If there were another way-"

"It's all right," she interrupted him. "I've known my fate for some months now. You're laird. As a woman of this family, I'm used as a way to negotiate peace through marriage."

Alistair tugged on her black hair. "I wanted you to be happy. I wanted you to have the kind of marriage our parents had."

"What about you? Don't you want that kind of marriage?"

He shrugged absently. "I doona believe I'll have that luxury. I'll broker my own marriage to another, stronger clan. But first, I must bring Donald to heel."

"If the men of Ravensclyde haven't already done it for you."

"Part of me prays they have," Alistair said in a low voice. "I doona relish fighting my own brother."

Both of them knew Donald wouldn't back down without a fight, and for Donald, who wanted to be laird, that meant to the death.

Innes knew the strength of both her brothers. Donald was good, but he often let his emotions get the better of him. Alistair was calm and cool during battle. He would win, but it would kill a piece of his soul in the process.

"We'll survive this," she stated.

Alistair gave her a crooked smile. "I'm going to ensure that you do."

~ ~ ~

He was famished. His stomach rumbled with the need for food as he inspected the cavern. As he thought, there was nothing but rock and torches. No water, no food. And no female.

At least he thought there was nothing until he spotted a sword leaning against the wall near the entrance. He smiled as he recognized his weapon.

He strode to it and wrapped his hand around the pommel. Then he grasped the sheath with his other hand and slowly pulled the sword free. A quick inspection showed that the blade was as sharp as he wanted it.

How could he remember the sword, but not recall how he came to be in the cavern?

The more he thought about it, the more his memories seemed to vanish before he could begin to grab them. He gave a shake of his head and sheathed his sword before he strapped it around his waist. It was time to go hunting for food.

He followed the only opening out of the cavern. He had to duck beneath the arch, and the tunnel was only marginally taller. Bent over, he had to navigate the winding and incredibly narrow passageway. Thunder continued to boom, and the rain grew louder the farther he walked.

Finally, he came to the end and was able to stand straight as he stood in a cave that opened out to the world beyond.

It was all gray, the rain blocking his sight of anything farther than ten feet ahead. So much for hunting. Food would have to wait. Water, however, wouldn't.

He walked out of the cave and lifted his head, eyes closed and mouth open to catch the rainfall. With every mouthful, the taste of the water was like heaven. He had no idea his throat was so parched, or that he ached to taste something so refreshing.

When his thirst was quenched, he lowered his head and returned to the cave. He paced, energy to get out and discover where he was coursing through him. He had to be in Scotland. The fates wouldn't be so cruel as to take him away from his beloved land.

The rain prevented him from seeing any landmarks with the rate in which it fell. The thick clouds stopped any shred of light from filtering through. And then night fell.

He sat in the middle of the cave staring out, watching the lightning zigzag between clouds in violent outbursts.

There was something he needed to do, people he needed to find, but he couldn't remember. All he knew was that he had to get out of the cave.

~ ~ ~

The castle was quiet in the pre-dawn hours. Only a few women were in the kitchen preparing the morning meal. Innes was on her way there when someone grabbed her from behind and clamped a hand over her mouth.

She struggled, kicking to no avail.

"Enough," a deep voice grated in her ear.

Donald. She stilled, anger filling her. How dare he treat her so roughly? And what was he doing back at the castle without Alistair's knowledge?

Donald was as tall as Alistair, but he had the barrel chest of their father. It was an easy feat for him to carry her up the stairs and down the hallway to the master chamber.

"Knock," he ordered her. "It's time we three had a talk."

If Donald had wanted to kill Alistair, he'd have already been upstairs and done the deed. That was the only reason Innes lifted a shaky hand and pounded on the wooden door.

A moment later, Alistair opened the door. His smile vanished when he took in Donald holding Innes. "What the bloody hell?"

Donald pushed his way inside. Only then did he release Innes. She hurried away, turning her gaze on Donald so he knew how furious she was.

"What is the meaning of this, Donald?" Alistair demanded.

Their brother closed the door and leaned back against it, his arms crossed over his chest. His kilt was dirty and his shirt was torn. His short hair was at odds with his dark bushy beard. "Did I hear right, Alistair? Are you going to reprimand me for doing what you should be doing, brother?"

"We have enough trouble. The last thing we need is to be at war with the Sinclairs, as well. Think!" Alistair said and pointed to his head.

Donald snorted. "I am thinking. Raiding is what we do in the Highlands. We need food."

Innes had heard enough. She stepped between her brothers and looked at Donald. "Going against Alistair so publicly is turning people against him – which is exactly what you want. We should be united to save our clan."

"I'm the answer to the clan," Donald said and swung his gaze to Alistair. "And he knows it."

Alistair's gaze narrowed. "This again? You willna be happy until you're laird."

"You doona see the bigger picture."

"And father did?" Innes asked angrily. "Is that why he snuck off in the middle of the night with only five men to take back our sheep?"

"Da led this clan with strength," Donald stated.

Innes nodded. "Aye, he did. He was also impulsive and rash, just like you, Donald."

Donald lifted his lip in a sneer. "You have the same blood running in your veins, sister."

"I do, but I learned patience from Mum." She swallowed and looked between her brothers. "I also learned that there is someone else who could be the answer to saving the clan."

Donald snickered and shook his head. "You're no' talking about that fool hidden away in the cave, are you?"

She blinked, blindsided that Donald knew about the man. Innes swiveled her head to Alistair to see his calm gaze on her. "You both knew? I thought I was the only one."

"Nay," Alistair said. "We've always known."

"Then why haven't you woken him?" she implored.

Donald waved away her words. "There's nothing he can do."

Innes was tired of the bickering between her brothers. It had begun the moment their father's body was returned to the castle. She crossed her arms over her chest and took a few steps back so she could see them both. "We'll see about that."

Donald's face mottled with rage. "I'll be the savior of our clan."

Innes could only gape when Donald threw open the door and stalked away. She glanced at Alistair, and then both of them hurried after their brother.

As Innes lifted her skirts and ran down the stairs, she glanced back to see Alistair strapping on his sword. She didn't have to ask to know that Donald was planning to kill her warrior.

The battle between brothers might very well

come sooner than she wanted. That was if Alistair intended to stop Donald from killing the man their family had protected for generations.

She wasn't sure of Alistair's intentions, and there wasn't time to ask. All she could do was hope that the amulet had woken her warrior as her mother told her it would.

CHAPTER THREE

He was thankful that the rain stopped by morning. For a moment, he thought it might continue on for another day. The storm had been fierce.

But as the sun peeked over the mountains, he stepped from the cave and smiled. Scotland. The mountains rose toward the sky, the bright green grass covering every inch. A ray of sunlight shone on the mountain so blindingly that he had to shield his eyes to be able to take in the view.

And what a view it was. Half the mountain was bathed in golden light, giving the grass a vibrant look that almost seemed unreal.

This was his home. The weather was unpredictable at best, and the same mountains looked different every day depending on the conditions.

He breathed easier knowing he was in Scotland. Now, he needed to find some food.

~ ~ ~

Innes caught up with Donald after they walked out of the castle, but her words were falling on deaf ears. Nothing she said halted him.

"You can't do this," she repeated when they reached the cave.

Donald chuckled, the sound devoid of humor. He didn't slow as he ducked and walked into the tunnel. "You'll realize you need to put your faith in me as soon as you stop thinking some dead man held in magic will help us."

"Never," Innes stated.

The tunnel was too narrow for Donald to turn around, but she knew anything could happen once they reached the cavern.

Except Donald stood still as stone when he reached it. Innes had to walk around him to see what had made him pause. When her gaze took in the empty slab, she could only stare in shock.

It worked! She had woken the warrior.

"Where is he?" Donald demanded as he swung his head to her.

Innes shrugged in bewilderment. "I've no idea."

Alistair's gaze lowered to her neck, and Innes knew the minute he noticed that her necklace was gone.

"You should've let me kill him here," Donald

said. "Now, I'll have to hunt him down."

Donald roughly pushed past her to retrace his steps out. She walked to the empty slab and placed her hands on it. If only she had waited a little longer, she might have been there when he woke.

"I wish you'd told me you were going to wake him," Alistair said from behind her.

Innes turned and lifted her gaze to him. "I didn't know that either of you knew about him. Mum told me to keep it secret."

Alistair shrugged. "It doesna matter now. We need to focus on stopping Donald."

Once more, Innes was running after Donald. This time she followed Alistair, who tracked their brother. When they came upon him, Donald was sitting on a fallen tree, his sword out with the tip in the ground as he braced both hands on it.

Innes was instantly on guard. So was Alistair, if the way he slowly circled Donald were any indication.

"You woke him, did you no'?" Donald asked in a soft voice.

Innes wasn't fooled. That tone of voice meant he was furious. She now wished she had gone back to the castle. How many times had she and Alistair chased after Donald when they were growing up? Sometimes they were able to talk him out of doing something foolish before he did it, but most times, they chased after him to get him out of trouble after the deed had been done.

Not until their father died did she see the real Donald, the man he kept hidden all those years. In his eyes, she saw that he would say anything, do anything to get what he wanted. Nothing and no one would stand in his way.

For the first time in her life, she truly feared Donald.

Donald got to his feet, his gaze never wavering from her. "Why did you have to do something so stupid?"

"It's done, Donald," Alistair said. "Leave it alone."

"I doona take orders from you," Donald said, briefly looking at Alistair. "Anyone who isna with me is against me. And our little sister just proved she was against me."

Alistair took Innes's hand and tugged her away. "Get to the castle."

She didn't want to leave her brothers. One of them was going to die that day, and she feared it just might be Alistair.

Innes turned to start running back to the castle when Alistair shouted her name. Out of the corner of her eye there was a blur of movement and then a grunt.

She slid to a stop and looked back to find that her warrior had effortlessly flipped Donald over onto his back. The warrior had his knee in Donald's neck and a dagger pointed between two ribs.

She met the warrior's gaze and marveled at eyes that were as blue as the sky. They stared at each other for long, silent moments until Donald began to struggle.

The warrior slammed a fist into Donald's jaw and knocked him unconscious.

~ ~ ~

He couldn't believe his luck when he heard the woman's voice. The rabbit he was hunting quickly forgotten, he followed the voices that led him to the cave. The woman wasn't alone though. Two men were with her, and by their looks, they were related.

Not wanting to be cornered in the cave, he decided to wait for their return. It didn't take them long. The first to exit was the burly man with the short hair and bushy beard. It wasn't long before the second man and the woman followed.

He followed them until they found the first man again. He'd known before anyone spoke that the bearded one was going to attack. At first he thought the man's assault might be against the other man, but when he realized his focus was on the woman, he refused to sit by and let it happen.

The moment the bearded man went after the woman, he jumped from his hiding place and took him down. He ignored the second man, his eyes locked on the dark-haired beauty with her olive skin and black eyes.

There was something about her coloring that triggered an emotion inside him. He felt as if he was supposed to be wary of it, but for the life of him, he couldn't remember why.

He had no idea how long he and the burly man

stared at each other before he finally had to knock the man out.

"Daman."

He jerked his head to the other man, a frown forming. Was that his name? How did he not know his own name?

"I'm Alistair," the man said. "Laird of the MacKays, and the man you took down is my brother, Donald. Thank you for that. I wouldna have gotten to Innes quick enough."

Innes. He found his gaze back on her.

Alistair cleared his throat. "I'm sure you have questions, Daman. Let's get back to the castle first."

He looked down at the man he had knocked out and slowly got to his feet. Innes had woken him, and Donald had been about to kill her because of it. Daman couldn't believe a brother would do that to a sister.

Daman could feel her closeness. He ached for her touch, but somehow he managed to keep his hands off her.

"Daman," she whispered. "I never knew your name."

He looked at her, drowning in the dark depths of her eyes. She was exquisite. Her black hair was thick and straight, the silky length hanging down her back. How he wanted to run his hands through it and have the strands drape around him as she leaned over him.

Daman took in her oval face, the clear complexion. Her lips were full and parted. Her eyes were wide and turned up seductively at the corners, giving her an exotic look.

Black brows arched elegantly over eyes that watched him. Unable to help himself, he reached up and gently traced a brow, just as she had done to him on many occasions as he slept.

Her eyes widened as her breath left her in a rush.

"We can no' tarry," Alistair said. "We need to get Donald to the castle and in the dungeon."

"How did you know Daman's name?" Innes asked Alistair.

Alistair glanced at Daman. "Mum told me."

It took both Daman and Alistair to lift Donald and half-carry, half-drag him to the castle. Daman had a difficult time concentrating on anything other than the woman walking in front of him.

Innes intrigued him, fascinated him. Captivated him.

With his gaze on her, he never saw the root. Daman tried to catch himself, but with the added weight of Donald he knew he was going to fall. He tried to call out and warn Alistair, but no sound passed his lips.

Daman fell hard to his knees, struggling to keep his hold on Donald and not let him fall. Daman tried to say Alistair's name again. Then he tried Innes's, but once again there was no sound.

His voice had been taken from him. He had memories of talking, so he knew at one time he could. Why had that changed?

"Daman?" Alistair asked. "Are you all right?"

Daman nodded and got to his feet. He lifted his eyes and saw Innes staring at him, her brow furrowed.

By the time they reached the castle, men were there to take Donald from him and Alistair. Daman gathered his breath as he looked around the bailey – a bailey that was nearly empty.

"Most of our people are gone," Alistair said sadly. "I'm losing my clan."

Daman looked into Alistair's dark eyes and shook his head as he frowned.

"It began a year ago when our feud with the Blair clan escalated to another battle. We faced a bitter loss that day with over half of our warriors dead or dying. While we made the trek home with our wounded, the Blairs raided the castle and took all our sheep."

Daman glanced at Innes to see her giving instructions to a couple of women.

"It didna take long for our food stores to run low," Alistair continued. "Soon, people began to leave. My father took a handful of men and tried to take our sheep back. He was killed in the process."

Daman took in the account and began to piece things together. Obviously, Donald wanted to be laird, but that was Alistair's role. How far would Donald go to get the title himself? Daman suspected he would do anything.

"Our clan chose Alistair as laird over Donald," Innes said as she walked up, confirming Daman's suspicions. "Donald hasn't forgiven Alistair for that. Or me for siding with Alistair."

Alistair wrapped an arm around Innes. "We've lost a lot of our clan because I'm unable to feed them. Donald gathered a following of men and took them to another rival clan, the Sinclairs, to raid them. In the process, many of those warriors died."

Innes leaned against Alistair's chest. "Donald has made an enemy of the Sinclairs that we don't need."

"War is coming," Alistair said. "And I doona have men to fight with me. I doona wish to battle the Sinclairs, especially when I know the Blairs are looking to take our lands. I need allies, no' enemies."

"That's where you come in," Innes said.

Daman's frown grew. Him? What was he supposed to do? Sure, he was a good fighter, one of the best actually. Was he meant to ride into battle with Alistair? If that was what Innes wanted him to do, then he would do it.

But they would fail.

It didn't matter how good a man was if he didn't have the forces behind him.

Alistair waved his arm around. "You're welcome here, Daman. I didna want my sister to wake you, but perhaps it was what we needed."

Daman followed them into the castle wondering just how much he would be willing to do for the lovely Innes. Then he knew the answer – anything.

CHAPTER FOUR

Innes couldn't stop looking at Daman. He was quiet, his bearing commanding even without speaking a single word. Without meaning to, he drew everyone's gaze.

She swallowed hard when he came to stand beside her in the great hall, his hand brushing hers. A spark zipped through her, primal and...erotic.

Then he looked at her.

His blue eyes were intense as they searched hers. Chills still raced over her skin from when he had traced her eyebrow. She wanted to ask him if he knew she had done that to him countless times, but she didn't have the nerve.

"You must be hungry," Alistair said. "We doona have much, but we'll gladly share what we do have."

Innes felt lost when Daman's gaze slid from her and moved to Alistair. He touched her brother's arm to get his attention. Once Alistair turned to him, Daman pointed to a bow and a quiver of arrows propped near the hearth.

Alistair frowned as he looked at the weapons then back at Daman. "You want to use them?"

Daman nodded and then walked to the hearth. He slung the quiver over his head, settling the strap across his chest. He lifted the bow and tested it by pulling the string back and looking along the sights. He lowered the weapon and caught Innes's gaze once again.

Innes realized then why Daman was so quiet. "You can't speak, can you?"

Daman's gaze briefly lowered to the ground before he shook his head.

Alistair asked, "Have you always been mute?"

Again Daman shook his head.

Innes wasn't sure she would be so calm if she woke after two hundred years without the ability to speak. Yet, Daman seemed entirely composed.

Daman pointed to Alistair and then the bow before he opened the castle door.

"You want to hunt," Alistair said, a slow grin forming.

Her brother hesitated, and Innes hurried to say, "I'll be fine. Donald is locked away, and we'll close the gates."

Alistair pulled on the end of her hair and strode away to get his bow and quiver. Innes looked back at Daman to find him watching her closely.

She noticed the silver chain around his neck that disappeared beneath his saffron shirt. Her necklace. The thought of it touching his skin made her stomach flutter in excitement.

If only she had been there when he woke. She would've had him all to herself for a time.

"We willna be far," Alistair said, breaking into her thoughts.

Innes jumped and jerked to her brother. "Of course. Be careful. Both of you," she said and looked at Daman.

Alistair exited the castle first. Daman hesitated before he gifted her with a smile and followed her brother. Innes walked to the doorway to watch them.

Her brother barked orders to the men standing guard at the gatehouse and those along the battlements. Alistair spoke while Daman nodded or pointed to something. It continued for a bit at the gate before they walked beneath the gatehouse. Alistair turned right, and Daman turned left.

Innes's heart jumped when Daman glanced back at her before disappearing beyond the gate. Only after the gate was closed and bolted did she shut the castle door and face the hall.

~ ~ ~

Daman returned to the castle with a deer and four hares. He would've hunted longer, but he couldn't shake the overwhelming need to get back to Innes.

The black-haired beauty was an enigma. All those times she had visited him, spoke to him...touched him. Her caresses had heated his blood, singed his skin. With the barest of touches, she made him crave more.

Now that he was awake, he wanted to yank her against him and taste her lips as he'd longed to do while he slept. She had no idea what her nearness did to him. She tied him in knots, and at the same time, she calmed a raging storm inside him that he hadn't yet figured out.

Right at the tip of his memory was the knowledge of something he was supposed to do, but every time he got close to figuring it out, it slipped further away.

The castle gates opened and Daman discovered Innes there to greet him. Her eyes lit up at the sight of the meat. It almost made him want to go back out and get more.

She took the hares from him as she said, "Alistair isn't back yet. You've made everyone very happy."

It was her bright smile that caused something in his chest to expand. Things were bad off at the MacKays. He wasn't sure what he was supposed to do, but he knew he would help in whatever manner asked of him.

As soon as he and Innes walked around the side of the castle to the kitchen, Daman saw the women. They were standing around, waiting for him. He shrugged the deer off his shoulder and laid it on the ground. Then he stepped back and let the women take over.

"Follow me," Innes said.

As if Daman would refuse. They passed through the kitchens and then up the stairs. He watched the sway of her hips and his cock hardened.

A memory flashed of brightly colored skirts. Then, just like that, it was gone again as if it never were.

Innes didn't halt until she reached the door to a chamber. She put her hand on the latch and waited for him. Her dark eyes held a hint of shyness, but there was curiosity and awareness, as well.

"You have no idea how much you've helped us today. Donald would've tried to kill Alistair, and though Alistair knows Donald needed to be brought to heel, he's still family. You saved Alistair that trouble and stopped Donald's attempt to take over the clan."

Daman didn't know what to say. He had only done what he thought needed to be done.

"Then there is the hunting. Alistair has put it off to search for Donald, but there is only so much one man can do. Thank you."

He didn't want her thanks. He wanted...her.

"Do you remember anything before you awoke?" she asked.

Daman nodded slowly.

"You remember why you were in that cavern?" she asked hopefully.

He hated to disappoint her, but he couldn't lie. Daman gave a swift shake of his head. How could he explain that he remembered instinctive things, but didn't know his name? It didn't make sense, even to him.

He knew he was formidable in battle and could wield a bow or spear as well as a sword. He knew he could ride a horse, steering the steed with nothing but his legs while charging into a fight so he could use his weapons.

Beyond that, there was nothing.

He wanted to ask her to help him figure it all out, but the words wouldn't come. Somehow, he knew that he'd never asked anyone for anything.

"There's a bath waiting," Innes said into the silence. "And food. It's the least I could do."

She started to walk past him, and he grabbed her hand. Her head jerked to him, her eyes wide. He placed his other hand over his heart and bowed his head.

Her smile was slow and sweet. "You're welcome."

He knew he should release her hand, but the feel of her soft skin was his undoing. His thumb grazed the top of her hand in slow circles.

When her lips parted and he noted the wild beat of her pulse in her neck, all he could think about was kissing her, of pulling her against him and feeling the warmth of her body as he held her.

He gently tugged her closer, his thumb still caressing her hand. She leaned toward him. Daman lowered his gaze to her mouth as he ducked his head.

He hesitated for just a moment, giving her time

to pull away. When she didn't, he touched his lips to hers.

The low moan that rose from within her had his body demanding more. He turned them both, pressing her back against the wall.

He kissed her again, adding more pressure. As soon as her lips parted, he slipped his tongue between them. Their tongues touched and danced while her arms wound around his neck and her fingers slid into his hair.

Daman deepened the kiss. The more he sought, the more she gave. Her kisses were seductive and innocent, enticing and wanton.

This was the woman who had awakened him, who wanted him to help her clan. The last thing he should be doing is assaulting her. Besides, it would not be good to have Alistair discover them like this after having been taken into their home. Daman needed to stop.

If he didn't stop now, he wasn't sure he would be able to later. His desire for Innes was that great.

He ended the kiss and pulled back. The sight of her kiss-swollen lips made him groan, but no sound could be heard.

Her eyes opened, blinking up at him dazedly. She touched her lips with her fingertips. "I have no words for how amazing that felt."

Satisfaction filled him. If only she knew how close he was to kissing her again.

He cupped his hands around her face and looked deep into her black eyes. Such beautiful eyes. They were so dark and deep that he could feel himself falling into them.

She lifted her lips to him, silently asking him to continue kissing her. Just as he began to lower his head, he heard Alistair's voice below.

Daman gave her a quick kiss and stepped away. When she didn't move, he turned her toward the stairs and gave her a gentle shove. Only when she began to walk did he go into his chamber and shut the door.

He sighed heavily. The kiss had been beyond his expectations. Innes was captivating, and she must have worked some kind of spell on him because he was bewitched.

A warning zipped through his mind, cautioning him to be wary. But as he tried to search the dark corners of his mind for why, he once more came up empty.

Daman removed his sword, boots, kilt, and shirt to walk naked - except for the necklace he still wore - to a wooden tub filled with water. It was still relatively warm. He scrubbed himself twice before he rose and dried off.

He touched the amulet around his neck. It was the same one he'd found in his hand when he regained consciousness in the cavern. If Innes was the one to wake him, did that mean this was hers? He knew it didn't belong to him.

Daman put his clothes back on and walked to the small round table and chair in his chamber. He sat and poured ale into a tankard as he looked at the trencher of food before him.

After the first bite of cold meat, he realized how

famished he was. It didn't take long for him to clean the trencher of every morsel.

He sat back to finish his ale as he looked around his quarters. It was a medium sized room. The bed sat against the far wall with bed curtains that were dark blue velvet. They were a little frayed, having seen better days.

It was more visible evidence that the MacKays were in trouble. Daman wasn't sure how they had lasted as long as they had.

With little food, very few men to hold the castle, and fighting within the family, they were ripe to be taken over.

Daman tried not to think of Innes, but he couldn't seem to help himself. That kiss had set him ablaze. The fire within for her had already flamed hot. Now, he burned.

Did she know how she made his blood heat? How he yearned to have her near? How he longed to hold her?

He thought she had been with him for decades, because that's what it felt like. But it was more like years. Just how long had he been in that cave?

Why was he put there? Innes and Alistair must know the answers. If only he could ask them. But that was rather hard without his voice.

He rose and began to pace the room. There were no memories. He responded to his name, he knew he could fight, and he knew he could hunt. Other than that, his mind was blank.

Except for the clawing feeling that he was supposed to be doing something.

Looking.

He latched onto the word. Looking. He was supposed to be looking. But for what? For who?

Daman squeezed his eyes closed and gripped his head. A dull ache had begun, settling in at the base of his skull. The pain grew until his entire head pounded.

It took him a moment to realize there was a second pounding – that of a fist against his door.

CHAPTER FIVE

Innes shifted in her seat in Alistair's chamber. She couldn't get comfortable. Ever since that scorching kiss with Daman, she'd been unable to think of anything other than him.

All through the evening meal she'd kept hoping he would come down, but Alistair had wanted to give him time. After the meal, however, Alistair waited until the hall cleared and then went after Daman.

Since neither she nor Alistair was sure of how many more of their people sided with Donald, they decided to keep their conversation private. There was nowhere more private than the master chamber.

Innes jumped when the door opened and Alistair filled the space. He gave her a frown and stepped aside. Then her gaze landed on Daman. Their eyes locked, held. It was a good thing she was sitting down because she was certain her legs wouldn't have held her after she saw the desire reflected in Daman's blue gaze.

"Thank you again for helping me hunt," Alistair said as he stopped at the hearth and turned to Daman.

Daman glanced down the hall before he closed the door behind him. He bowed his head and crossed his arms over his thick chest as he leaned against the wall.

Alistair clasped his hands behind his back as the fire popped behind him. "I wish things were no' so dire for us. I was none too pleased that Innes woke you, but now I think she did the right thing."

Innes saw Daman's slight frown, his hesitation, as if he were trying to figure things out. There was something about the way the lines bracketed his mouth that made her think he was in pain.

She held up a hand to stop Alistair before he continued. "Daman, do you know why you were in the cave?"

He shook his head slowly.

Innes frowned. "That part of the story was lost to us. I was hoping you would remember. All we've been told was that you would one day save our clan."

Daman held her gaze for a moment before his blue eyes slid to Alistair and he shrugged.

"Aye, I didna think you would know that either," Alistair said with a sigh. "The truth is, you doona have to do anything. Our family has kept watch over you for two hundred years."

Was it Innes's imagination, or had Daman jerked at the mention of the time that had passed?

Alistair continued, saying, "Now that you're awake, you can do whatever you wish. Nothing holds you here."

Daman pointed to Alistair and then to Innes.

Innes glanced at her brother. "Daman, you don't owe us anything."

"She's right. You doona," Alistair said. "But I'm asking if you'll stay and help us fight if needed. Now that Donald is no longer a worry, I must turn my attention to the Sinclairs. They want a meeting."

Innes swiveled her head to Alistair, shocked. This was the first she had heard of it. "What?"

Her brother pulled out a rolled missive from the sleeve of his shirt. "This arrived before the evening meal. David, the laird of the Sinclairs, wants to meet at our border. He is bringing the Lord of Ravensclyde with him."

"And his army, no doubt," Innes said tightly. "The Sinclair doesn't want to talk. He wants to fight."

Alistair tucked the missive back up the sleeve on his left arm. "David is an honorable man, Innes. I believe him. I was hoping Daman would accompany me."

Daman was nodding even as Innes asked, "When is this meeting?"

"In the morn."

She closed her eyes in despair. Her world was truly crumbling around her. If only Donald had stood with Alistair instead of against him.

"I would like you there as well, sister."

Innes's gaze snapped open to look at her brother. If he wanted her with him, that could only mean one thing – a marriage proposal.

She couldn't pull a breath into her lungs. They were frozen with dread. How could she possibly go to another after having Daman with her?

After his kiss?

She was being selfish, but that didn't stop the feeling from continuing. The lives of her brother and her clan rested with her. She could broker peace if she were willing to be the bride of the Sinclairs' laird.

Innes had known her fate for years, even if she hadn't known which man she would marry. Why was she rebelling now?

"I sent a missive to The Sinclair two days ago," Alistair said into the quiet, as if reading Innes's thoughts. "He was willing to meet, but now that Donald has attacked, I doona know where we stand."

She tried to swallow, but her mouth was too dry. "Give him Donald. Let the Sinclairs exact their justice."

"I'm sure they will want that, but Donald is family. I'll punish him myself."

Daman shook his head and looked pointedly at Innes.

She shivered, remembering the fury she'd

witnessed in Donald's gaze before Daman intervened. Donald would've killed her.

"Hmm," Alistair said. "Good point, Daman. But Donald willna be leaving the dungeon so he can no' hurt Innes." Alistair walked to the round table near the hearth and motioned Daman over. "I've made a map of our land, as well as where we border with the Sinclairs and the Blairs."

Innes watched as Daman strode to the table and braced his hands on the wood as he let his gaze wander the map. Occasionally, he would point to something. Alistair would then explain the area in detail.

While the men studied the map, Innes kept thinking of marriage. She touched her lips, her stomach fluttering as he recalled how Daman had turned and trapped her between him and the wall.

Chills raced along her skin as she remembered the feel of his lips – firm and eager – and the way he'd held her.

As if there were no tomorrow.

In some ways, there wasn't. Not for them.

Innes waited until both men were too engrossed in the map and their planning – Alistair talking and Daman either nodding or shaking his head – to notice her before she got up and quietly exited the chamber.

She made her way back downstairs to the kitchen. Innes pushed up her sleeves and began helping a few others clean up from the meal. More and more people left the clan every day. Pretty soon, it would only be her and Alistair.

She stopped washing dishes as it hit her. No, she wouldn't be with Alistair, she would be with her new husband far away from here. Her marriage would foster peace between the Sinclairs and MacKays. That also meant that Alistair would have the backing of the Sinclairs.

It would be enough to keep the Blairs away. The Sinclair clan was the strongest around. No one went against them. The support of the Sinclair clan would allow Alistair to find himself a wife and procure another ally. Hopefully their people would return by then.

It was the only way to survive.

Why then did it feel as if she were doing the wrong thing? Why did it feel as if her place was to remain right where she was?

Innes was so conflicted. She wanted to help save her clan, but she also wanted Daman. The way he looked at her, it was as if he knew her. Which was silly, since they'd just met. She had been visiting him every day for years, but he didn't know that.

Did he?

Innes finished the washing and dried her hands. She walked from the kitchen as Daman was coming out of the solar, his head swiveling as if he were looking for something.

As soon as he spotted her, he walked to her and took her hand. Excitement coursed through her when he laced his fingers with hers. She lifted her skirts with her free hand and followed him up the stairs all the way to the battlements. She sucked in a breath when the cold air hit her.

Daman turned to face her as he pulled her against him. His heat enveloped her, wrapping them in a cocoon of warmth. He gently touched her face with first one hand, then the other. One hand slid into her hair and around to the back of her head. His gaze was intense, the desire palpable.

There were no words needed between them. The passion was too great, the need too forceful.

She rested her hands on his chest and wished that there were no clothes between them. She ached to be pressed skin against skin. Everything she thought, everything she *was* centered upon Daman.

His eyes lowered to her mouth a heartbeat before he kissed her.

Innes wrapped her arms around his neck and melted into him. It wasn't a soft, learning kiss like the one from before. This one was full of fire and heat and longing. And her body responded instantly.

He deepened the kiss before she could right herself, sending desire pooling in her belly. Before Innes knew it, she was pressed against the battlement wall by Daman's hard body.

She ran her hands over him, touching every part that she could. There wasn't a part of him that was soft. Just steely muscle beneath her palms.

Her head dropped back as he kissed down her throat. Innes didn't know such passion existed, but now that she did, there was no way she could marry another.

Cool air hit her legs a moment before Daman's large hand hooked beneath her knee and yanked her leg up. Innes gasped at the feel of his hard arousal pressed against her.

In the next instant, she was holding air. She grasped the battlement and lifted her head to search for Daman. He was standing against the back battlement wall, his face contorted with regret and need.

Innes knew she couldn't go to her groom anything but an innocent, but it wasn't him she was thinking about. It was Daman and how she felt in his arms. Nothing mattered but this moment.

She held out her hand to him, but Daman gave a rough shake of his head and drew in a shaky breath.

"I don't care what Alistair has planned," she said. "I don't want this to stop."

Daman's blue eyes flared with desire. He slowly looked her up and down, his intent clear. If he kissed her again, there wouldn't be any stopping him.

Innes crossed the distance until she stood in front of him. "I don't want you to stop. Ever."

He cupped her face and stared at her as if his world had just been ripped to pieces.

"I've waited years to have you open your eyes and see me," she said. "I've tasted your kisses, felt your desire. Don't take that away."

He jerked his head behind him, indicating the castle and clan.

Innes licked her lips and shrugged. "Everything

I have ever done has been for the clan. I'm not thinking of anyone or anything other than me and you right now."

Daman looked as if he wanted to argue the point more. Then, he released a deep breath as his frown disappeared. He gave a nod. Once more, he slipped his hand in hers. Together, they faced the battlement door and walked back into the castle to his chamber.

As soon as the door closed behind them, Innes was once more yanked against him in a fierce kiss that took her breath away.

CHAPTER SIX

Daman was shaken, staggered.

Stunned.

With every kiss, every touch, Innes sank deeper into his soul. He knew he shouldn't be with her since she was promised to another, but he couldn't walk away. He had to hold her, just as he had to take his next breath.

She had become the center of his world.

He didn't wonder why or worry. He simply accepted the fact.

Innes grounded him in a way he couldn't understand. Even the knowledge that he had been asleep for two hundred years wasn't enough to send him away. Because without her, without her soft voice and beautiful, dark eyes, he knew he would go mad.

She was the only one who spoke to him while he was in the cave.

She was the only one who touched him as he lay sleeping.

She was the only one who penetrated the darkness, giving him...hope.

She was the one who awakened him.

Daman ended the kiss and leaned back to look at her. He wished he could tell her how she gave him a reason to live. He wanted to tell her that her beauty left him breathless.

More than that, he desperately wanted to tell her that she healed the raw, aching wounds deep inside him with only a smile.

He didn't know what plagued him, what made him think he had something to look for. Only that he instinctively knew that he did. It ate at him constantly. But Innes eased his soul, soothed his heart.

She didn't make him forget what gnawed at him. Instead, she made him believe that he would eventually do all that was needed of him.

"No one has ever looked at me like that," Innes whispered. "You make me want to blush and believe I can fly all at the same time."

He could make her feel like that just by looking at her? Daman had never experienced anything like it before. If only he could speak. Then he would tell her of all the feelings inside him. The biggest one? Hope.

Daman didn't know why that one stood out. Was hope absent before? As soon as he began to search his mind for memories, the headache returned.

Innes immediately frowned and smoothed her hands over his face. "I don't know what's troubling you, but don't think of it now."

Nay, now wasn't the time for it, not when he had Innes in his arms. Daman dropped his hands to her hips and began to gather her skirts. There was a shyness and innocence about her that made him feel protective – and strong.

He pulled her dress over her head, but before he could reach for her shift, she dropped to her knees and pulled off his boots one at a time. When the second one hit the floor, Daman pulled her up and backed her to the bed. He couldn't help but grin when he saw the desire in her gaze.

He gently pushed her down so she sat on the bed, then it was his turn to take off her boots. After he'd removed them, he placed his hands on one slender ankle and slowly ran his hands up her calves to her thighs.

Her chest rose and fell rapidly, her lips parted. She braced her hands behind her on the bed, leaning back just enough. She had no idea how difficult it was to clamp down on his control and not cover her body with his right then.

Daman began to roll down her stocking. He hadn't realized until that moment how sexy a stocking could be, but being able to caress her skin as he rolled them down made his cock ache with need. Her second leg was just as erotic. By the time he finished, they were both panting and needy.

Daman stood and unpinned his kilt. It fell to the floor at his feet. Innes sat up and slid her hands beneath his saffron shirt.

Innes sucked in a breath at the feel of his skin beneath her palms. It was great to touch but she wanted to see, as well. She shoved the shirt up. Daman jerked it off and tossed it aside, leaving her gaping at the specimen before her.

He was simply...glorious.

Every inch of him was honed with muscle. She took in the sight of his wide chest, the rippling sinew of his stomach, and his thick arms.

Then she looked down at his arousal jutting out between them, thick and hard.

He placed his finger beneath her chin and lifted her gaze to his face. She stared into his blue eyes for several moments before he bent and kissed her.

In an instant, she was flat on her back, his delicious weight covering her. The world blurred and faded as she lost herself in the kiss – in Daman.

He rolled onto his back, taking her with him. She was so lost in the kiss that she didn't realize he was taking off her shift until he briefly ended the kiss to pull the garment over her head.

His hands were everywhere, stroking, learning, caressing. It felt...right.

She was surprised when he pulled her knees up so that she straddled him. Then he sat her up. Innes gazed down at him, her hands braced on his chest.

Daman took in the sight of her, wondering if

she knew just how stunning she was with her dark hair falling around her in disarray, her lips swollen, and desire in her gaze.

His cock jumped, his balls tightened.

His heart clenched.

How could he have such a woman in his arms and let her go on the morrow? He couldn't. He knew it in his bones. Innes was his. If he had to fight a hundred armies, he would. Just to have her as his.

Daman cupped her breasts and ran his thumbs over her nipples. Her eyes slid closed as a sigh left her lips. He rolled her nipples between his fingers as her head dropped back, causing her long hair to brush his thighs and cock.

He teased her nipples mercilessly until soft cries left her lips. Her hips began to rock as she dug her nails into his chest. When Daman could take it no more, he sat up and latched his lips around one turgid peak.

Her hands grasped his head as she moaned low in her throat. Daman suckled first one breast and then the other as their bodies rocked against each other.

He could feel her arousal, and it drove him mad with need. In a blink, he flipped her onto her back and slid a hand between their bodies to the dark curls that hid her sex.

Daman gritted his teeth when he felt how wet she was. He gently slipped a finger inside her. Her legs parted as her hips rose up to meet his hand.

He removed his finger and began to slowly,

lightly circle it around her clit. Daman inwardly smiled when he heard her breath catch and felt her body melt into the bed. Her chest heaved as her cries grew louder, her moans longer. He alternated between teasing the swollen nub and thrusting a finger inside her.

She was shaking, her body close to release. But he wasn't finished with her yet.

Daman scooted down her body until he was nestled between her legs. Then he placed his lips on her.

She whispered his name, her hands fisting in the blanket. Daman watched her as he licked and laved her clit, ruthless in his desire to give her pleasure.

Never had he felt such need to sink into a woman, to claim her. He couldn't wait to fill her and have her legs wrap around him.

The only thing that dulled the moment was the reminder that she wasn't his. Alistair intended her for another. Daman briefly wondered if he should refrain from claiming her as he yearned to do and simply give her pleasure.

Then she climaxed and coherent thought left him.

Daman watched the ecstasy cross her face, felt her body shake with the force of the orgasm. He rose over her, his cock poised at her entrance.

Innes opened her eyes as the amazing bliss began to recede. Her body still pulsed. She blinked up at Daman, only belatedly realizing that he was no longer touching her.

His jaw was clenched, and there was a question in his eyes.

There was only one answer for her. Innes wrapped her hand around his arousal, amazed at how hard it felt, yet at the same time, the skin was as soft as velvet.

She brought him to her entrance. There was a moment where surprise flickered in his eyes, then he slowly entered her.

The feel of his thickness stretching her while he gradually thrust deeper and deeper inside was exquisite. Their gazes were locked as their bodies joined again and again until he met her maidenhead.

She clung to his shoulders, unsure of what came next, but ready all the same. He pulled out of her until just the tip of him remained, then he tugged her knees up and plunged inside her.

Innes gasped at the pain when he breached her innocence. She squeezed her eyes closed, surprised that he remained still until the worst of the pain was over.

She once more opened her eyes to find him watching her. He gently touched her face, as if asking if she were all right. It amazed her that Daman could be so powerful and strong, yet gentle at the same time.

A smile pulled at her lips as she nodded. The corners of his mouth tilted in a grin. Then he began to move again.

Innes was swarmed with pleasure. It consumed her, overwhelmed her, and she welcomed it because it was Daman who brought it out in her.

His hips began to move faster, driving him deeper, harder. She was swept along, her body eager for more. Sweat slickened their bodies as she wrapped her legs around him and locked her ankles.

She began to lift her hips to meet his thrusts. He might not be able to talk, but his face conveyed his pleasure better than words ever could.

All too soon, he grunted and pulled out of her. She held him tightly as his body jerked. It wasn't until she felt something on her stomach that she realized he hadn't spilled his seed inside her.

They remained there for a long time before Daman rose and found a cloth. He wet it with a pitcher of water and then returned to the bed, cleaning off his seed and then the blood of her innocence from between her legs.

Innes couldn't remember the last time someone had taken care of her like Daman did. It just proved how different he was, and why she didn't want anyone but him.

She watched as he cleaned himself. When he finished, he dropped the cloth, pulled back the blankets and raised a blond brow. He wanted her to stay. It made her heart want to leap from her chest with joy.

Innes got beneath the blanket and then found herself pulled back against his chest as he reclined against the headboard, his arms around her.

They sat in silence for long moments, but she hated that she couldn't see his face to see what he was thinking. She held no regrets. She hoped he didn't either.

Regardless of what was to come, this night was hers. She'd made the decision to be with Daman and have some joy when no other decision had been hers to make. No one and nothing could take that away from her.

Just as no one could take Daman from her.

CHAPTER SEVEN

Daman was wondering how in the world he would be able to watch Innes leave with David Sinclair? He wasn't sure he could.

Nay. He knew he couldn't.

He was prepared to fight Alistair and the Sinclairs for her. That's how much she meant to him, even before he had marked her as his.

"I don't regret this," her sweet voice broke the silence. She turned to face him, her brow furrowed slightly. "I don't want you to either."

He shook his head as he smiled.

Innes chuckled as her shoulders drooped. "Good."

Daman tugged at the ends of her hair, amazed at the thickness and how it felt like silk in his fingers.

"When you first saw me, you looked as though you knew me."

He nodded and touched her lips.

"You heard me talking to you?" she asked in surprise, her dark eyes wide.

His smile grew as he gave another nod.

"Did you hear others before me?"

He'd only ever heard her. Daman shook his head, his smile dying.

"I knew when Mum showed me to the cave and I saw you that you would change my life," Innes said. "I just didn't realize how much."

He laced their fingers together, grateful that he couldn't talk because he had no words. She claimed that he had changed her life, when in fact it was the opposite. Innes had given his life back to him, and in the process, had given him something to fight for – her.

Daman placed her hand over his heart. He didn't fully understand the feelings churning inside him, but he recognized that he hadn't felt them for another woman. Regardless of the life he'd once had, he knew there hadn't been a woman before Innes.

Nor would there be one after her.

She blinked rapidly and lowered her gaze. "For all eternity, you will be in my heart, Daman," she whispered.

He pulled her back against his chest and wrapped his arms around her. Long after Innes had fallen asleep, Daman's mind went over every scenario in which he was allowed to keep her. And every one of them ended in battle.

The hours ticked by steadily, as if fate were set against him. He watched the sky lighten through the slit in the shutters.

An hour before dawn, Daman looked down at Innes sleeping in his arms and felt his heart tighten in fear. He couldn't lose her. Without her, he would be lost.

He touched her face, letting the pad of his finger skate down her cheek. She woke gradually and finally her eyes opened. Her smile was radiant when she looked at him.

Up until she saw the sky.

"You shouldn't have let me sleep. I wanted more time with you," she said, her voice laced with regret.

Daman stopped her when she started to rise. He had no way of asking her if she would consider remaining with him. He could only hold her, hoping she saw the need in his gaze, felt the longing in his embrace.

"I must get to my chamber before Alistair finds me gone," she whispered and gave him a lingering kiss.

She was out of his arms in the next instant, her dress hastily thrown on as she gathered the rest of her things and reached for the door. She paused and looked over her shoulder at him.

Then she was gone.

Daman wanted to hit something, to scream his fury. If only he had friends he could seek out. It would be the first time he asked for help, but he was willing to do anything for Innes.

~ ~ ~

Innes stood in the bailey stroking her horse's forehead when she heard the voices from within the castle. Alistair was bellowing, and suddenly, everyone was rushing about.

She looked to the castle entrance as the door was thrown open and Alistair emerged followed by Daman. Her heart dropped to her stomach like a stone. Had Alistair discovered that she had given her innocence to Daman?

Daman's gaze was a mixture worry and anger as he looked at her, his hand resting on the hilt of his sword. But that fury wasn't directed at Alistair.

"Someone released Donald," Alistair told her in a tight voice as he walked down the castle steps.

Innes looked around at the faces of her clan. Those who remained had left the village and taken shelter at the castle. One of them was responsible.

"Who did this?" she asked them as she came around her horse. "Do you want to see another clan take over the castle? Because that's what is going to happen. Who would dare to go against your laird and free Donald?"

No one bothered to respond, and it infuriated her.

"Do you have any idea what Alistair and I have done for you? Do you even care? Perhaps we should let the Sinclairs take over," she said, her voice failing at the end.

She had been willing to give herself to the Sinclair laird for peace, but her clan didn't want peace. Why should she wreck her life for people who didn't care?

Innes felt a presence beside her and knew it was Daman. He turned her away to lead her back to her mare. His strong hands wrapped around her waist, and she looked into his eyes.

His long hair was tied back in a queue, giving his stark features more of a dangerous look. His blue gaze sought hers. Then he gave her a slight nod.

Innes took a deep breath. "I'm all right."

At that, he lifted her onto her horse and walked to his own. Innes didn't look back as she and Daman left the castle with Alistair.

They hadn't gone far from the gatehouse before she said, "Perhaps we should just keep riding and forget the clan."

"Nay," Alistair said. "They're my responsibility."

"They freed Donald," she stated. "I think that says everything."

"We doona know who freed our brother, but it wasna the entire clan," Alistair argued.

Innes snorted. "The fact is, someone did. Someone went against you and released him. We don't know who supports you and who supports Donald. I fear we won't know that until Donald challenges you again."

Daman was riding ahead of them, his gaze sharp. Innes thought of the previous night and waking up in his arms. If only every day could be like that. Was it too much to ask that she be allowed to be happy? That she be able to choose a husband for herself?

"Do you love him?"

She was pulled out of her musing by Alistair's question. Her eyes swung to him. "What?"

"I'm no' blind, Innes. I see how you look at him. More importantly, I see how protective he is of you."

"I woke him."

"Aye. But I think there's more you're no' telling me. I want things to go smoothly today. In all ways."

She looked forward, her gaze landing on Daman. "You mean you want to know if I'll refuse to go with the Sinclairs."

"That's exactly what I mean."

"Have I given you any reason to doubt me?"

Alistair was quiet for a long time before he said, "No' until now. Our clan needs peace, Innes."

"Then give them Donald," she argued. "They know he's the culprit."

Alistair blew out a breath. "We must all make sacrifices for the clan."

Innes felt tears threaten. She was a laird's daughter. She knew better than to cry over things out of her control. It didn't make it any easier to swallow, however.

~ ~ ~

Ravensclyde Castle

Stefan sat atop his horse outside the gatehouse looking toward the border between the MacKay and Sinclair lands. The missive from Alistair MacKay had been a surprise, but a smart one, nonetheless.

A horse and rider sidled up next to Stefan. He didn't need to look over to know it was Morcant. He, Morcant, and Ronan had been up since before dawn scouting the castle for signs of another attack.

David believed the MacKay laird, but the three of them were not so inclined.

"What are you thinking?" Morcant asked.

Stefan looked over at his friend and rubbed his jaw. He didn't want to be meeting with a laird. He wanted to be out looking for Daman. The four of them had been cursed by a gypsy two hundred years earlier. Ronan had been the first out of his dark prison, with Morcant second out of his. Stefan had arrived just a few days ago.

All three of them had been drawn to Ravensclyde. They refused to believe it was coincidence, which is what gave them hope that Daman would be found soon.

"Stefan?" Morcant asked with a frown.

"I'm thinking of Daman."

Morcant nodded. "I had hoped Leana would have a vision about him."

It wasn't only Morcant's wife that had special

abilities. Morvan was a child of the forest, able to help animals in a way no other could – and she was all Stefan's.

"We only got to visit a few places on Sinclair land before we were called back to Ravensclyde," Stefan said. "He could be out there waiting for us."

Morcant shifted atop his horse. "I doona expect our meeting with The MacKay will take long. Once everything is sorted as David wants, we can get back to our hunt."

"It was three months between Ronan getting out of his prison and your arrival."

"We'll find him, Stefan."

None of them ever talked about the possibility that Daman hadn't been cursed with them. Daman hadn't gone into the gypsy camp with them initially, and he didn't have the flaws the rest of them had. The only thing Daman had a problem with was asking for help.

The sound of horses approaching from behind alerted Stefan that it was time. Ronan and David drew even with them, and the four of them headed out to the border.

By marrying Meg Alpin, the cousin of Laird David Sinclair, Ronan had become Lord of Ravensclyde. It still boggled Stefan's mind how he, Ronan, and Morcant had made a life for themselves after being cursed.

"We willna be going to war, lads," David said.

Morcant glanced at him. "I'll be prepared either way."

"David believes Alistair MacKay," Ronan

repeated Morcant's earlier words. "The marriage will bring peace."

Stefan frowned as he glanced at the young laird. Without the two hundred year difference in their ages, David would be around their age. He was intelligent, brawny, and fierce as only a Highlander could be. "Nay. Only Donald MacKay locked in our dungeon will bring peace."

"If Donald acted alone," Morcant added.

David might believe the MacKay laird, but by Ronan's tight lips, he was prepared for war, as well.

"I doona make agreements lightly," David said and pinned Stefan with a look, his dark gray eyes intense. "I learned the truth of the MacKays. Donald is trying to oust his brother for control. Alistair is doing what any good laird would do. He's saving his clan."

"And you're willing to take a bride you've never met?" Ronan asked.

David smiled, though it was forced. "I doona have the same luxury as you three to marry someone I love. I'm laird. I marry for alliances."

"I wouldna think the MacKays are much of an alliance," Stefan said.

"Their land borders mine," David said. "If the Blairs decide they want the MacKay lands and holdings, I'll have to prepare to go to war with them. The Blairs take whatever they want, and I'll no' have my people put through that. Most of the MacKay clan has come to us. Once they realize the MacKays are allied with the Sinclairs, and Alistair has ensured Donald can no' cause any more trouble, the people will return to the MacKays."

Morcant nodded and said, "Alistair will once again have soldiers to hold off the Blairs."

"As well as my men," David added. "I'll be married to his sister."

CHAPTER EIGHT

Daman wanted to pretend he couldn't hear the conversation between Alistair and Innes, but it was impossible. He felt her pain and it infuriated him that he couldn't help her as she needed. All Daman could do was fight and kill. He was damn good at it, too.

If he couldn't stop Alistair from handing his sister over to the laird of the Sinclairs, then all Daman could focus on was watching out for Donald.

The middle MacKay wasn't just loud and abrasive. He was obvious. Daman hadn't bothered to mention that Donald would show up at the meeting because Alistair already knew, and there was no sense in putting an added worry on Innes.

Daman may not have been part of a family, but

even he knew that to go against a brother as Donald had Alistair was beyond terrible.

Donald had put everyone at the castle at risk, and he didn't seem to care. All Donald wanted was power. He was an idiot. It took more than brawn to lead a clan.

Daman had learned that from...

His thoughts went blank and his head began to throb dully. He ground his teeth together against the pain as the realization hit that he had almost remembered something. But what?

And who was he thinking about?

Need to be looking.

Daman gave a shake of his head. His thoughts were jumbled, his mind swimming with an urgency he couldn't elude. He was supposed to be looking for something.

Or was it someone?

He glanced over his shoulder at Innes. He had already found her, so she couldn't be it. Was it Donald? Nay, he was just a troublemaker. Besides, Daman didn't know of him until he woke.

Whatever pushed Daman had been with him for a long time – possibly as long as he had been asleep.

"We're no' far," Alistair said.

Daman licked his lips, wishing he could ask Innes specific details. If he could only talk, he might find out what he was supposed to be searching for. She might even know more details of his past.

A warning tickle pulled him out of his thoughts

and focused him once more on his surroundings. They came to a river, and Daman waited for Alistair and Innes to cross before he followed.

He glanced behind him as the hairs on the back of his neck rose. Someone was watching them. Donald most likely, but how many men had Donald brought with him?

Once across the river, Daman nudged his horse into a gallop and caught up with Alistair. He motioned with his head behind him as Alistair's gaze landed on him.

The laird of the MacKays frowned. "Donald?" he whispered.

Daman lifted one shoulder in a shrug as he set his hand atop the hilt of his sword. Alistair then moved his horse over and motioned Innes forward.

Finally, they reached the border between the MacKay and Sinclair lands. Daman saw a man sitting atop a large gray stallion. The man had light brown hair hanging to his shoulders and a full beard. His gaze was focused on them, looking each of them over. With the way he sat confidently and with a commanding presence atop his mount, he was obviously the Sinclair laird.

They came to a stop with ten feet separating the groups. Daman then let his gaze move to the rider next to the laird. The man's horse pranced in agitation. Daman looked into the man's face to find the Highlander staring at him intently.

Daman frowned as the man refused to look away. He watched Daman as if he knew him, which was impossible. The man couldn't know Daman, he had just been awakened after two hundred years of sleeping in a cave.

Daman inwardly snorted. Two hundred years. The passage of time was mindboggling, but it was the knowledge that someone had put him there that really caused anxiety. He had no recollection of anyone or anything that would explain that, and neither did he have time to think on it at the moment.

"David," Alistair said. "Thank you for meeting with us."

David bowed his head. "Attacking your clan didna seem right after so many have left."

"My brother will be punished," Alistair promised.

David glanced at Innes. "Where is Donald?"

Daman once again narrowed his gaze on the man next to David. It was obvious he was a warrior, a man trained with a sword. No wonder the Sinclair laird had brought him along.

If Daman were David, he would have brought more warriors. Daman had wanted Alistair to bring more men. The problem was, there weren't enough left.

"As of last night, he was in our dungeon." Alistair sighed. "Unfortunately, someone released him."

"Does he know of this meeting?" the man next to David asked.

David motioned to him. "Alistair, this is Ronan Galt, Lord of Ravensclyde. He is married to my cousin, Meg."

Alistair nodded to Ronan in greeting. "No doubt Donald knows of this meeting. It's why I've brought Daman along as extra protection for my sister."

"Where did Daman come from?" Ronan asked.

Daman tensed. Why would he ask such a question? Wouldn't anyone assume Daman was part of the MacKay clan?

"He has always been with our clan," Innes stated in a clear voice.

Her leg brushed Daman's as her horse shifted, and it was all Daman could do not to reach over and take her hand, to pull her onto his horse and claim her lips.

Ronan looked from Daman to Innes and back to Daman. There was something about the way Ronan stared that agitated Daman. If he could talk, he would demand that Ronan state whatever bothered him.

"You look like a capable warrior, Daman," David said.

Daman glanced at the laird.

"He is," Alistair answered. "He's already taken Donald down once."

"Why can he no' tell us this himself?" Ronan asked.

Innes pinned him with a scathing look. "If you must know, he can't talk."

"He can no' speak?" Ronan repeated with a deep frown furrowing his forehead.

"I didna think we were here to talk of Daman," Alistair said. "I thought we met to talk of peace."

David nodded slowly. "That we did, Laird. Innes, did your brother tell you the terms?"

"He did."

Her voice wobbled, causing anger to rise up within Daman. She shouldn't have to make such a sacrifice because of Donald's mistakes. Daman's grip on his sword tightened.

"Are you in agreement?" David asked her.

Innes hesitated. Daman could feel her gaze land on him briefly. "I've always been willing to do what was needed for my people."

"But?" Ronan pressed.

"She has nothing else to add," Alistair stated with a meaningful glare directed at Innes.

Tension filled the area as David and Alistair watched Innes while she looked at the ground. Daman and Ronan were once more locked in a stare.

"Well now, is this no' cozy," Donald said as he walked out of the brush behind them, the blade of his sword resting against his shoulder.

Daman whirled his mount around, unsheathing his sword. He was about to charge Donald when Alistair said his name. Daman looked at the laird, waiting.

"What are you doing here?" Alistair demanded of his brother.

Donald chuckled. "You know why I'm here."

"You can't win against the Sinclairs," Innes said. "Why would you want them as an enemy?"

Donald merely smiled. "I never said I wanted them as an enemy. What I wanted was for our clan to see how weak Alistair is. I needed our people to see that I'm the only one who can protect them?"

Daman lifted his lip in contempt. *Protect.* Donald didn't know the meaning of the word.

"That's why you tried to kill Innes?" Alistair demanded, his voice lowering in his anger. "We had enough trouble with the Blairs, Donald. If you had stood beside me, we could've stolen our sheep back and fed our people. Your so-called plan sent our people away and gained us a potential enemy in the Sinclairs."

Donald lowered his sword until the point was in the ground and set both of his hands on the hilt. "I've got my men with me, Alistair. Who do you have? One man who is supposed to save our clan? He willna last against my men."

Daman swung a leg over his mount's head and slid to the ground. He gently shoved the horse away.

"Nay, Daman," Alistair said. "This is my fight."

Innes tried to dismount, but Daman was too quick. He kept her atop the horse and gathered the horse's reins beneath its chin. He then turned the horse toward the Sinclairs.

"Daman," Innes whispered.

He looked up into her dark eyes. Gypsy eyes. Why hadn't he noticed that before? She had the same coloring as a gypsy. It was exotic and beautiful.

And deadly.

Where had that thought come from? Daman shoved it aside and drank in her features. She had to be kept safe. There was about to be a bloodbath, and the only ones who could keep her out of it were the Sinclairs.

Daman turned to David and raised a brow in question. David nodded once. Daman walked Innes and her horse over the border and handed the reins to Ronan.

"Daman," Innes said again, louder this time.

He turned his back to her and returned to MacKay land. Alistair and Donald were already circling each other, their swords drawn and at the ready.

Donald was the first to attack. The clang of swords was loud in the quiet. Alistair easily blocked the swing and sidestepped, knocking his shoulder into Donald. Donald stumbled backward, his lips twisted in rage.

Alistair was quick, his attacks calm and on target. Donald let his emotions rule him, causing him to miss Alistair several times. Daman began to relax when it became apparent Alistair would win. Donald cut Alistair's arm, but Alistair turned away before it could go too deep.

Donald attacked again. Alistair didn't turn away this time. He met his brother's attack and used Donald's force to turn him slightly so that Donald fell on his back.

Alistair put the point of his blade at Donald's throat. "Call your men out here."

"Nay."

"It's over, brother," he said and kicked the sword out of Donald's hand. "I've defeated you, and since I can no' trust our people no' to release you again, I'm going to hand you over to The Sinclair."

Donald's dark eyes blazed with hatred. "You'll have to kill me."

Alistair lowered his sword and took a step back. "I'm no' spilling the blood of my brother. Everyone here saw your defeat."

Daman couldn't be happier. Alistair's actions proved he was meant to be laird. The best thing to do would be to kill Donald, but Daman understood why Alistair hadn't been able to.

Daman was walking toward them when Donald reached for his boot. Daman opened his mouth to call out to Alistair, but there was no sound. Daman rushed to Donald, but Donald had already risen to his feet and plunged a dagger into Alistair's back by the time Daman reached him. Daman could hear Innes screaming.

Daman slammed into Donald, sending him crashing to the ground. Daman knelt beside Alistair and cradled his head as he looked into the dying man's eyes.

"Doona let him rule," Alistair said. "Doona let him hurt Innes." Then he issued his last breath, his eyes closing.

Daman gently laid Alistair down and gathered his sword as he stood. He pointed to Donald's sword with his own, waiting for Donald to pick up the weapon and face him.

As soon as he did, Daman attacked. He swung his sword in wide arcs as metal met metal time and again. Donald was taller by a few inches, but he didn't have the skill Daman did.

Daman blocked Donald's sword countless times. He kicked Donald and slammed his elbow into his face, which only caused Donald to become angrier. His swings went wide as his emotions took over.

He waited for Donald to get close and then plunged his sword into the man, feeling it sink deep into Donald's body. Surprise showed on Donald's face, as if he couldn't believe he was dying. Daman then shoved Donald off his blade and turned around.

"Daman!" Innes shouted as she came running at him.

CHAPTER NINE

Daman gathered Innes in his arms and held tight, turning his face against her neck. She had lost both brothers that day. Daman should have paid closer attention. He might have been able to save Alistair.

"It's not your fault," she whispered, her hands stroking his head. "Alistair should never have turned his back on Donald."

Daman opened his eyes to find Ronan and David watching them. A moment later, two more men rode up beside Ronan. Daman released Innes and pushed her behind him as he glanced over his shoulder to see if any of Donald's men would attack. There were just two men who walked out from behind trees to stand over Donald and Alistair's dead bodies.

There was no doubt Daman could take Ronan and the others. He would rather do it after Innes was back at the castle, but he doubted David would allow her to leave.

David's lips compressed for a moment. "What a waste," he said. "Alistair was a good man. That was quick thinking, Daman."

Innes stood behind him, her hands gripping his tartan. Daman gave her a push. But just as he thought, she wouldn't leave.

"Daman has always been quick," Ronan said.

David grunted. "So you told me."

Daman looked between the two before his gaze shifted to the newcomers. One man had sandy blond hair and yellow-brown eyes while the other had light brown hair and hazel eyes. Their gazes were a mixture of shock, surprise, and happiness.

"Daman," said the man with the blond hair. "You know us."

He snorted and shook his head. He didn't know these men.

"He doesna recognize us, Morcant," said the second man.

Daman took a step back. He needed to get Innes to safety. There was no way he was turning her over to David Sinclair. Not now. Not after she had lost her family.

"Where have you been?" Ronan asked. He nudged his horse and guided it across the border onto MacKay land. He drew up before getting too close. "We've been looking for you. It's been a long time since the gypsy camp."

A flash of brightly colored skirts in the grass flashed in Daman's mind a heartbeat before an old gypsy woman's face, her dark eyes filled with anguish and fury.

Ilinca.

The name sprang into his mind, but Daman knew that was the old woman's name. She was a witch. A gypsy witch. She was the one responsible for putting him in the cave and having him sleep for two hundred years.

He hated gypsies for what she had done.

Daman jerked his head to Innes to see her dark coloring. Gypsy. He squeezed his eyes closed and turned his head back to Ronan.

Ronan slowly dismounted from his horse and dropped the reins. It made Daman frown because he had seen Ronan do that action before, he just didn't know how or when. Somehow, Daman also knew that he had picked up the reins from Ronan afterwards.

"It was my fault," Ronan said. He ran a hand down his face. "I can admit that now. I should never have gone to see Ana those times. I was the one who urged the three of you to accompany me," he said, motioning from Daman to the other two men.

Ronan cleared his throat. "You were the smart one. You remained outside the camp."

Daman closed his eyes as his head felt like it was splitting open. He grabbed it, doubling over from the agony. As if from a great distance, he could hear Innes calling his name. It took Daman a moment to realize he had fallen to his knees.

More flashes of faces and events filled his mind in rapid succession. He opened his mouth and tried to bellow, to ask someone for help, but there was only silence and the roar of pain.

Three pairs of large hands gripped him, steadying him. Daman kept his eyes closed for fear of letting in any light that might make the throbbing worse.

He saw Ronan, laughing as he put his arm around a dark-haired woman with bright skirts. Those same skirts he had seen lying in the grass. With blood.

Ana.

Daman felt something tighten around his chest, cutting off his air. He fought to fill his lungs with air even as an image of Morcant held immobile by Illinca filled his mind.

Then there was Stefan. The rage he dealt with constantly taking him over. In a blink, all three of his friends – his brothers – were gone. Illinca had used her magic to curse them.

All of his memories returned in a tidal wave, drowning him in sorrow, happiness, anger, and hope. And just like that, the pounding in his head stopped and the constriction around his chest eased. Daman remained still for a moment.

"He's no' rocking anymore," Morcant said.

So the three of them were holding him. Daman lifted his head, intending to talk to them. But all he saw was David holding Innes who had tears coursing down her face as she shouted his name over and over.

Daman threw off his friends' hold and jumped to his feet. How he wanted to demand that David release Innes. No sooner had the thought entered his head, than the words left his mouth.

Everyone stilled.

Innes blinked at him. She shrugged out of David's hold and took a step toward him. "You spoke."

Daman reached out and pulled her against him. "Aye. I can speak again."

"What happened to you?" she asked with a sniff.

Daman leaned back. He gazed into her dark eyes before he looked over her head to David. Then he turned his head to the side to where Ronan, Morcant, and Stefan stood.

How many times had his friends told him that asking for help wasn't a sign of weakness? To him, however, it was. Illinca had taught him the importance of asking for help by taking away his voice.

"I remember. Everything." He drew in a deep breath. It felt great to be able to speak again. It felt even better to see his friends.

Now he knew why he'd had that unshakable feeling of needing to search for something. He was meant to look for Morcant, Ronan, and Stefan.

Instead, they had found him.

"Everything?" Stefan asked.

Daman nodded. "I saw her curse each of you. I saw each of you disappear. I crossed into the camp, and she used her magic to keep me still. She said she'd had a vision, knew we would be there, but she hadn't seen Ana's death."

"I still say Illinca needs to die," Morcant mumbled.

Innes's head jerked toward Morcant. "Did you say Illinca?"

"What of her?" Ronan asked.

"She's the grandmother of one of my ancestors, Amalia. Amalia brought Daman to our land and married the MacKay laird."

Stefan scowled. "Are you telling me that you were no' in a dark prison, Daman?"

"I was asleep," he answered. "I woke in a cave. It was Innes who pulled me out of my sleep."

Innes touched his cheek. "It was foretold that he would save our clan."

"So he has," David said. "Alistair couldna kill his own brother, but Donald didna have such morals. With Donald dead, the MacKays will need a new laird. I think you've found him, Innes."

Daman saw her smile as she looked at him. He shook his head. "I'm no' a leader."

"You always have been," Ronan said. "You just didna want to take the role."

Daman faced his friends. "I couldna remember any of you. I knew I was missing something, but I couldna figure out what it was."

Morcant was the first to enfold him in a hug and pound on his back. Daman was smiling when Morcant stepped away, his head down as he brushed something from his cheek.

"Leana is making him soft," Stefan said right before he pulled Daman in for a hug. "It's good to have us all together again."

Then it was Ronan's turn. Daman couldn't be happier. Until he saw David. His smile vanished as he faced the laird.

"I know you and Alistair had an agreement," Daman began.

David held up his hand and grinned. "I doona have to ask Innes what she wants. I saw it in the way she couldna get to you fast enough. I wouldna dream of coming between the two of you."

"I'm sure you've heard things you didna understand today," Daman said.

David laughed and mounted his horse. "I know all about Ilinca's curse and the four Highlanders she bound. It's been a story told for generations in my family. Why do you think we had the mirror Ronan was trapped in?" he asked before he turned his horse around and rode away.

"Will you help me with Alistair's body?" Daman asked his friends.

The four draped Alistair across his horse. Daman wasn't surprised to see Donald's two men cart Donald's body off into the forest. He knew their faces, and he wasn't sure he would allow them back onto MacKay land.

That's when he stopped his train of thought. It wasn't his land.

"What next?" Innes asked him.

He looked down at her. Her eyes were still red from her tears. He wanted to ask her to be his, but it wasn't the right time. She needed to bury her brothers.

"We bring Alistair back home."

Innes nodded and turned to Ronan, Morcant, and Stefan. "You are welcome to come with us."

Us. Daman wrapped an arm around her, feeling more free than he ever thought possible. The only way things could get any better was if Innes agreed to be his wife.

He inwardly smiled. Wife. It was something he hadn't ever considered, and yet as soon as he had woken, that's all he had thought about. Well, not so much making her his wife but remaining with her. It was all the same in the end.

EPILOGUE

Three months later...

Innes was holding her cheeks, they hurt from laughing so hard. It was only a few months since Alistair's death, but Daman had helped her heal in ways he would never know.

Donald's body had never been recovered. Neither were the two men who freed him from the prison, which was fine with her.

Just as she'd assumed, the clan eagerly accepted Daman as their laird. Whether he knew it or not, he had the commanding presence, intellect, and warrior mentality that made a great laird. People recognized that.

In the months he had been laird, there wasn't just peace with the Sinclairs. He, Ronan, Stefan, and Morcant, along with a handful of MacKay men, stole back the sheep the Blairs had taken.

The Blairs tried to steal them again, but Daman had been prepared for them. The Blairs now knew that the MacKays weren't a clan to be messed with. Retribution would be swift if they did.

Daman's laughter rang out in the hall as Meg elbowed Ronan in the stomach. Innes had heard each of their stories of how the men were cursed and how they came to be in this time. Their stories of finding love were even more interesting.

Innes had slept in Daman's bed every night since returning to the castle. She wondered how much longer he would take before he asked her to be his. She was growing tired of waiting.

"I hated Ilinca," Stefan said. "My first thought was to kill her when I realized I was out of the darkness. I still hate her. Some," he added as he looked at Morvan. "She did bring me to my woman."

Morcant lifted his goblet. "To our women. Even I'll thank Ilinca for that."

Innes watched as Daman smiled and lifted his goblet with the others, but he was restless. "What is it?" she leaned over and asked.

He shook his head.

Innes knew him well enough to know the look pinching his lips. He was worrying over something.

She rose and sat on his lap. When his gaze met hers, she touched his face. "I wonder, Daman, if you know that I love you."

"Aye, lass. I know," he said, his face softening.

"Just as you know I love you."

It was the first time he had said the words. She did know it by the way he touched her, treated her, and the way he spoke to her. But a woman needed to hear it all the same.

"Then when are you going to ask me to be yours?"

He tugged at her long, dark hair. She had left it free because he had asked her to. "I wanted to give you time. You lost both of your brothers in one day."

"All I ever need is you."

Daman set his goblet down on the table and cupped her face with his hands. "Innes MacKay, yours was the only voice I heard in my sleep. Yours was the only touch I felt. As soon as I woke, all I wanted was to find you. Even without my voice, we were able to communicate. With a voice or without, I'm no' me without you.

"I wasna going to let David have you that day. I didna care if I had to fight thousands of armies. I was willing to do it to have you by my side, to have you as mine. From the first moment you spoke, from the first time you touched me, I've been yours."

Innes felt the tears spill down her face. Daman's face swam in her vision as she listened to his words.

"Be mine. For now and always. Will you consent to be my wife and rule this clan beside me?"

Her throat was clogged with emotion. All she

could do was nod, and then he was kissing her.

Gypsies, magic, curses, and love. Innes didn't know how Ilinca knew the four Highlanders would bring about such change in the clans, and it didn't matter. The men were there, and the women who fell in love with them were willing to stand with them no matter what the future held.

Daman had saved the MacKay clan. He had also saved her. That last bit might not have been in the prophecy, but Innes didn't care. She knew the truth in her gypsy heart.

"Marry me. Right now," Daman said between kisses. "I've had the priest waiting for weeks."

Innes laughed as she jumped up and started running out of the castle toward the chapel. She didn't get very far before Daman grabbed her hand.

Then they were in the chapel, surrounded by friends – family, really – as they became husband and wife.

"My wife," Daman said with a smile.

"My rogue."

Look for the next LaRue story – **MOON THRALL** – Coming April 13, 2015!

It was the smell of bacon frying that pulled him from sleep. Court threw an arm over his eyes to block out the light coming through the row of windows behind him.

"This is beyond anything I've read in years," his brother Kane said.

There was a thud that Court recognized as Kane firmly setting down his mug of coffee. Court released a breath, hoping to fall back asleep quickly. It wasn't going to be easy when Kane was sitting at the table six feet away.

"What now?" Riley asked.

His cousin from Lyons Point had been sharing Kane's apartment for weeks now, and it looked like she had no intention of leaving anytime soon.

"This...well, there's no other way to put it. It's shit," Kane grumbled.

Court sat up and glared at both of them. It was wasted since Riley was focused on cooking and Kane was absorbed in reading the paper.

"It's too damn early in the morning for this," Court said as he rose from the couch and shuffled into the kitchen. He palmed a mug and poured himself some coffee.

Riley chuckled as she munched on a slice of crispy bacon and eyed him. "It's not early for us."

"Perhaps if you got in at a reasonable hour,"

Kane said as he set down the paper. "Besides, tell me again why you aren't at *your* place?"

Court took two sips of coffee and let the caffeine settle in his stomach before he replied. "It's not my fault the women won't leave me alone."

"You might try not sleeping with the nut jobs," Riley stated and pulled out the last of the bacon before she dumped eggs into the pan and began to scramble them.

Court frowned as he looked at the food, feeling a little jealous that he was missing out on such a delicious start to the day. "Do you cook for Kane every morning?"

Kane sat back in his chair. "Sometimes I cook."

Riley shot Kane a smile. Court hadn't been sure anyone could bring Kane out of his funk after the chaos that happened in Lyons Point when he had been cursed and sent after Lincoln's woman. Riley was doing what no one else could.

Kane wasn't his easygoing self – yet. But he was getting there. He didn't snap at people as often, and Court even saw his mouth easing into what could almost be a smile more and more.

"This," Kane said, pointing to the newspaper, "is stupidity at its finest."

Court leaned back against the counter and scratched his bare chest. Kane read the paper religiously every morning. While everyone else had moved into the modern age and either didn't bother to read the paper, or read it electronically, Kane was still old school.

Riley dished out eggs onto three plates. She turned to the table with plates in each hand and waited as Kane folded the paper so that the article was on top. Riley set the plates, as well as the bacon and biscuits, on the table. She motioned for Court to sit as she gathered utensils and napkins. Court hurried to put on his shirt from the night before.

She was the last to take her chair at the round table. Then she looked at Kane and asked, "What did you find?"

"An article on the supernatural in New Orleans."

Court shook his head as he cut open his biscuit and slathered it with butter. "That's nothing new."

"It is when this reporter is going to clubs were the supernatural visit and writing about it."

Riley choked on her coffee. She wiped her mouth with her napkin, her eyes wide. "Are you serious?"

Court watched Kane nod his head of golden blond hair. "It's just a piece in the paper. No one is going to read that drivel, and even if they do, no one will believe her."

"It's not the article that has me so upset," Kane stated around a mouthful of eggs. "It's that she points out the factions and describes some of the leaders perfectly."

Court waited until he swallowed his bite before he asked, "Who is described?"

Kane leaned over the paper and read, "Though tattooing has always been appreciated in our fair city, there is a faction who likes to tat their heads.

These beings should be steered clear of at all costs."

"At least she recognizes the Djinn are dangerous," Riley said.

"People are going to be heading out to the Viper's Den and Boudreaux's looking for these tattooed people."

Court realized that Kane had a point. "How long is the article?"

"Long enough." Kane stabbed the eggs with his fork for a bite and held the utensil at his mouth. "This is her third article, so I don't expect it to be her last."

Riley swallowed the last of her biscuit while she held another piece of bacon in her hand. "Perhaps I should go have a talk with her."

"That would be a bad idea." Court pushed his clean plate away and scooted down in his chair as he leaned back. "If we go to her, she'll know that we know something. I don't want to be mentioned in any of her articles."

Kane's lips twisted in revulsion as he chewed. "Her first articles merely mentioned the supernatural part of the city. It seemed harmless enough until this morning. She's visiting these bars, Court. If she's not careful, she's going to die."

"That's what we're for." Riley smiled when they turned to her. "I say 'we' because I have been helping out."

Court stared at his beautiful cousin. Riley had long black hair and the same blue eyes that all the Chiassons and LaRues had. She was tall, lithe, and had a smile that could make the Devil beg her take over Hell itself.

He understood all too well why his four male cousins in Lyons Point had done everything in their power to keep her away from the monsters they hunted. What Riley's brothers didn't understand was that she was stubborn and completely immovable when she focused on something she wanted.

There was no way Riley wasn't going to help them whether it was hunting a rogue vampire, or protecting a human getting too close to danger. All the LaRues could do was make sure that Riley never went out alone. One of them was always with her to watch her back.

Because none of them wanted the Chiassons descending on New Orleans because Riley got hurt.

Thank you for reading **The Seduced**. I hope you enjoyed the story as well as all of the Rogues of Scotland! If you liked this book – or any of my other releases – please consider rating the book at the online retailer of your choice. Your ratings and reviews help other readers find new favorites, and of course there is no better or more appreciated support for an author than word of mouth recommendations from happy readers. Thanks again for your interest in my books!

Donna Grant

www.DonnaGrant.com

Never miss a new book
From Donna Grant!

Sign up for Donna's email newsletter at
www.DonnaGrant.com

Be the first to get notified of new releases and be eligible for special subscribers-only exclusive content and giveaways. Sign up today!

ABOUT THE AUTHOR

New York Times and *USA Today* bestselling author Donna Grant has been praised for her "totally addictive" and "unique and sensual" stories. She's written more than thirty novels spanning multiple genres of romance including the bestselling Dark King stories, *Dark Craving, Night's Awakening,* and *Dawn's Desire.* Her acclaimed series, Dark Warriors, feature a thrilling combination of Druids, primeval gods, and immortal Highlanders who are dark, dangerous, and irresistible. She lives with her husband, two children, a dog, and four cats in Colorado.

Connect online at:

www.DonnaGrant.com

www.facebook.com/AuthorDonnaGrant

www.twitter.com/donna_grant

www.goodreads.com/donna_grant/

17967332R00069

Printed in Great Britain
by Amazon